ANGEL
SONGS

ANGEL
SONGS

20 Christmas Short Stories
and Poems, *plus* Recipes

DONA WATSON

Runewood Press

Editor: Beverly Nault
Cover image: © philcold/dreamstime
Runewood Press logo artwork: © Olivier Le Moal | Dreamstime.com

ISBN 978-0615908298

Published by:

Runewood Press
http://runewoodpress.com

To Steve,
Who always helps to make Christmas
just a little more magical.
I love you.

CONTENTS

THE ERRANT ELF

Brianna tugged the hem of her green vest and straightened her pointed hat, jingling the little bell on the tip. Even though she had to juggle a few things to fit this into her schedule, handing out Christmas presents to the third grade class was not something she wanted to miss.

When her husband's job had transferred them cross-country, this became Amber's third new school since kindergarten and the young girl was having a harder time adjusting with every new group of friends. Brianna had volunteered to be homeroom mom, hoping her participation would help her daughter adjust.

The holiday party was Brianna's idea and the other parents were so busy they were happy to let her do all the work, gladly chipping in a few dollars each for twenty-two stuffed Beanie Buddies. When Mr. Belvedere agreed, her creative mind had gone into overdrive and while she admitted that perhaps she had gone a bit overboard with the costume and wagon, it'd be worth it to see the kids' faces. And maybe Amber would finally be accepted as part of the class.

She opened the back of the SUV and her friend's Great Dane, Diesel, greeted her with a sloppy lick, his tail whipping from side to side. Brianna's breakfast toast took a turn in her stomach and she wrinkled her nose, reaching for a towel to wipe herself dry. Clipping a leash on his collar, she coaxed the enormous dog out of the vehicle and tethered him to the bumper so she could strap costume antlers on the animal's massive head. Stepping back to admire the instant reindeer, she congratulated herself on her brilliant idea.

Turning back to the SUV, she grabbed the handle of a high-sided red wagon borrowed from the next-door neighbor and eased it out, gently lowering the front two wheels to the ground, then with a grunt, the back two. She pulled out the makeshift harness fashioned from webbed tie-down straps nabbed out of her husband's pickup truck, and settled it on Diesel's shoulders, buckling it securely around his chest and ribs and then fastening the straps to the wagon. Now for the giant red bag she'd made and filled with Beanie Buddy plushies. She wrested it out and plopped it into the wagon with an *oof!* then slammed shut the back of the vehicle.

Brianna double-checked to make sure everything was in place and smiled. Short of having an actual elf, reindeer and sleigh, this was the closest she could get to the real thing and, truth be told, she was pleased with how it all came together.

She untied the leash, looped it around her wrist and turned toward the school building, then paused. Santa's reindeer never wore collars with leashes. She looked over the dog, who stood calmly, regarding her with bright eyes. Might as well make it look as authentic as possible.

She unclipped the strap from the dog's collar and dropped it into the wagon, then wrapped her fingers tight around Diesel's collar as if it were a suitcase handle. She smoothed down her vest one last time and started across the parking lot toward the school buildings, the jingle bells on her hat and ankles announcing her approach.

Halfway across the lot, an orange tomcat stepped out from behind a car and when it saw Brianna and Diesel, froze. The dog immediately came to attention, feet planted, head up, ears forward. Brianna sucked in a breath and adjusted her grip.

"Steady, boy."

She could feel his muscles tense, his head crane as she clenched his collar with both hands and tugged, but the giant stood his ground, gaze glued on the paralyzed cat.

"Come on, Diesel, this way," she coaxed but instead of obeying her, the dog growled at the coiled cat, who bolted, breaking the spell. The Great Dane lunged after it, jerking free of Brianna's grip. She stumbled a few steps after the dog, grabbing at the wagon as it whizzed by.

Brianna helplessly watched the Great Dane bounding away, red wagon and presents bouncing merrily along behind, barely missing car bumpers and a bike stand on its way around the lot. Puffing air through her bangs, she sprinted after the dog, glad the wagon was heavy enough it didn't seem in danger of turning over. If only it were heavy enough to stop the dog from—

Up ahead, the orange tabby blur streaked across the parking lot and over the curb, the Great Dane in hot pursuit, the wagon lurching over the concrete barrier onto the green lawn.

"Diesel! Wait!" *Ding ding ding!* Jingling bells announced her pursuit and she caught the green hat as it fell. Except for the bells, it was part of her daughter's Legend of Zelda Link costume, and if Brianna harmed it, she'd be toast.

With the dog's strides swallowing footage with every step, the only thing preventing the dog from closing the gap between was the wagon that bucked and rolled, slowing his gallop. In desperation, the cat veered out into the road, and antlers flopping, Diesel followed it into the middle of the street, pacing the speeding cat.

Then, to Brianna's horror, a car turned onto the street heading straight toward them. She sprinted into the road, waving her arms wildly to warn the driver.

Jingle jingle jingle. The bells on her ankles grated on her nerves with every step, and worse, only spurred the animals on. When a woman pushing a baby stroller stopped to watch her run past, a thought occurred that perhaps the bells might not have been the best idea.

The driver's gaze darted from the speeding animals to the panic-stricken Brianna and one corner of her mouth twitched up in a grin. She stopped the car and hopped out as the terrified feline ran onto the grass and dove into a thick privet hedge. Panting, tongue lolling to the side, Diesel jumped the curb and the wagon careened to one side, launching two Beanie Buddy frogs from the bag. The Great Dane thundered up to the bushes, skidded to a stop and jammed his head into the foliage, snuffling after the cat. Several frantic strides later, Brianna caught up to the dog and seized his collar.

Scooping up the errant frogs, the driver trotted over and handed them to Brianna. "Are you okay?" She tucked a long blond strand behind an ear.

Brianna nodded, gasping. "Thanks." She shoved the elf's hat back on her head, its jingle bells mocking her every move.

"Glad to help." The woman backed away from Diesel, slime rolling off his tongue, and returned to her car, chuckling all the way.

Thoroughly humiliated, Brianna retrieved the leash from inside the wagon and hooked it onto Diesel's collar. He looked up at her with the biggest doggy grin possible, eyes sparkling. She straightened his lopsided antlers and tugged gently on the leash. Now properly secured, the dog responded readily.

"Come on, boy," she ordered. "Let's get going. We have presents to deliver."

Checking her watch, Brianna trotted back to the school, dog in tow. They paraded past the receptionist, who greeted them with a surprised expression, and down the hall to Mr. Belvedere's classroom, stopping just outside windows that looked out onto the hallway. Twenty-two little faces turned her way, eyes round and bright. The teacher looked up and took in the sight, then grinned and rushed over to open the door. Brianna could feel her face flushed red with the exertion of the chase and she wished she could have taken a moment to wipe her brow.

She knew her elfin demeanor was a bit disheveled when one of the man's eyebrows twitched up and he spoke in a whisper, "Is everything okay?"

Brianna nodded and dry-swallowed, wishing she had a big glass of water.

Mr. Belvedere held the door open wide, then turned to the class. "Look, children! There's someone here to see us!"

A murmur of young voices and excited "Look at the doggie" whispers filled the air. Still panting happily, Diesel pulled the wagon in and stood dutifully calm, now on his best behavior.

One by one, she called the children up to the front of the room and handed each one a plushie. Every child petted Diesel as they walked by, their beaming smiles priceless, new treasures held tight.

"You're lucky your mom is so cool, Amber," one of the kids said.

"Yeah," said another. "My mom would never bring a dog to school."

Maybe the makeshift reindeer wasn't such a bad idea after all, Brianna thought. She rubbed a sore shin, waiting for the last student, her own daughter, to come forward but her heart fell when she saw her daughter's frown.

"Mom, when you came to the door, the other kids giggled," Amber said in a whisper, "I was kind of embarrassed."

Brianna studied her daughter's face, worried she might have made things worse. Then something she hadn't seen since they'd moved to town months ago warmed Brianna's soul, making the entire morning worth it as Amber's face morphed into a big smile. "But you were great." Throwing her arms around Brianna's neck, Amber kissed her over-rouged cheek. "Thanks, Mom. This is going to be the best Christmas ever!"

❄ ❄ ❄

ANGEL SONGS

"Monica, honey, try to keep up."

"But I'm tired, mommy. And my feet hurt."

"That's okay, baby. We're almost done." Monica's mother hurried just ahead of her toward another store, her brother Chad walking alongside carrying two bags by the handles. Carolers on one side sang "Silent Night" but the crowded mall was anything but silent. Four teenage girls strolled by, chatting and laughing. Shoppers hurried in every direction, intent on finding the last few perfect presents before Christmas morning dawned in seven days.

In all the noise and excitement, Monica barely heard her mother's reply. The five-year-old slowed to a stop in front of the toy store and pressed her nose against the cool glass of a display window, awed by the miniature Beauty and the Beast scene on the other side. The Beast stood by a little Christmas tree, handing a wrapped gift topped with a red bow to a smiling Belle seated on the divan. There was a real chandelier and a fireplace, and on the mantle, the tiniest little nativity set. The characters were just about the right size for Monica's dollhouse and she imagined how much fun it would be to play with them.

Both hands pressed to the glass, she gazed at the scene until her breath fogged up the window, then reluctantly turned away to catch up. But when she looked down the wide hallway, her mother was gone, swallowed up into the teeming mass of shoppers.

"Mommy?" Monica spun around the other way, but she wasn't there either. Just a mall full of strangers hurrying past. Tears welled up in her eyes as she stood frozen, frantically trying to think of what to do.

"Are you okay?"

Hearing the voice behind her, Monica turned and looked up into a pair of the kindest, green eyes. A man dressed in army clothes knelt down on one knee.

"What's the matter, little one?"

Monica was tempted to run but then remembered a warning her mom had made her repeat: *If you're ever lost, find someone with a nametag or a mommy with happy children and ask them for help.* This army guy had a nametag. "My mommy..." Monica tried not to cry, but her little chin quivered nonetheless.

"Don't cry." His gentle voice calmed her. "I'm sure she's not far. Why don't we wait here for a minute and see if she comes back? I'm sure she'll be looking for you."

Monica sniffled and wiped her nose on the back of her hand while the soldier stood and took her hand, turning toward the display window.

"Did you see Belle?" He pointed at the tiny figure robed in a billowing yellow gown.

"Uh huh." Monica eyed the little present, wondering what could be inside.

"Did you see baby Jesus up on the fireplace?"

She looked at the manger scene, then up at the man. He gazed at the crèche and smiled, his voice soft and low.

"Have you ever wondered what it would have been like to be there? Seeing the angels and then, best of all, baby Jesus?"

Monica had never thought of it before and she looked at the little barn with the angel above it, hands extended. "Did the angels really sing?"

"Oh yes," he looked down at her with moist eyes. "They sang."

"Was it loud?"

One corner of his mouth raised in a grin. "It's hard to describe. There's nothing like angel-song. What a night that was."

Just then, he knelt down and turned her toward the direction where she had last seen her mother.

"Look, is that your mom?"

Monica's heart flooded with relief to see her mother heading toward her at a fast walk, Chad trotting along behind her, shopping bags bouncing against his legs with every step. Her mother shot a worried gaze from side to side, eyebrows scrunched together, lips pressed tight.

Monica pulled a finger from her mouth. "I think she's gonna be mad."

"No." The soldier patted the top of her head. "I don't think so. I think she'll be pretty happy to see you."

Just about that time, Monica's mother spotted her and a smile washed over her face. Monica rushed into her mommy's arms.

"Oh, Monica, darling. I was so worried about you." She drew back and looked at her closely. "I'm so glad you stayed here and waited for me to come back. There's a smart girl."

"The soldier told me to wait."

"The soldier?" Monica's mother looked first one way and then the other. "Honey, I don't see a soldier."

"But he's right there." Monica turned to point him out, but stopped. He was gone. She stood and stared at the place where the man had been just moments before. "He was right there."

"Are you playing make-believe again?" Her mother wrapped Monica in another tight hug until she struggled to breathe. "If you'd stop all this pretending, then you wouldn't get lost, honey. Now let's go." She took Monica by the hand and set off back down the hallway toward the next store.

Monica glanced over her shoulder to the figures of Mary, Joseph, the angel, and the baby on the miniature mantle. She thought of the soldier's words and wished she could have been there at the stable to hear the angels sing.

Monica followed her mom into the perfume store, wondering where the soldier went so fast. She wanted to ask him more about the pretty music and the baby Jesus.

Just then, the mall carolers broke out into a soft chorus. Monica knew this song. She'd heard it at church.

Angels we have heard on high, sweetly singing o'er the plains...

WHITE CHRISTMAS

Snow

Falling free

Quiet, pristine, pure

Frosts tree, bush, rock and fence

Painting town, mountain, and field

Hearts at peace, at home.

White Christmas

Dreams

CHRISTMAS TREASURES

Eric screwed up his face and squinted across the frozen valley. The bright sunlight on the snow stung and filled his eyes with tears. He figured it'd take nearly all day to reach the other side, twice as long as it used to. A cough racked his frame until his whole body ached and he paused to catch his breath. The malamute at his side whined and he patted the animal's head with a gloved hand.

"Come on, Tundra. Won't get there standin' here all day." The dog nudged his hand in reply.

Eric clutched his walking stick with a resigned grip and headed down the slope. The dog pulled a small sled, scratching over icy rocks behind them.

Snow crunched under worn boots, moisture seeping in through the holes until his feet were numb. And still he plodded on. If he remembered correctly, it'd be Christmas Day soon. He thought of all the Christmases past. He and his brother had been inseparable then, especially when their parents moved them west. Ma had taught them from the Bible and Pa had taught them to be a team. But those years were long gone.

A few hours later and the sun high overhead, Eric paused in a small clearing. Leaning heavily on his walking stick, he brushed the snow off a fallen log and eased his weight down onto it, sighing in relief. Tundra looked on, head cocked to one side. Without a word, Eric slung the satchel from his shoulder and dug out the last slab of venison jerky. He ripped it in half, offered one portion to the husky and tore a bite off the other. Within seconds, Tundra's hunk was gone and the dog licked his whiskers, eager for more.

Chewing slowly, Eric took in the sights. A bright red cardinal flitted from one tree to the next, landed on a branch overhead and called out a song. Sunlight sparkled on the surface of the snow until every inch gleamed. Once he made it down the mountain, Eric wondered if he'd ever have the strength to climb back up again. With a sigh, he poked the last bite into his mouth, collected his things and started off again. Still a couple hours to go.

Eric slogged through the drifts all afternoon. As the daylight waned, he topped the last rise and looked down the gentle slope at the two-story house he and Sarah had moved into with his older brother and her sister all those years ago. Back then it'd been fun—two brothers marrying two sisters—and they'd been the talk of the town. But now sorrow twisted his gut like a knife to see the place where they had been so happy together...and the place where Sarah had died. Below in the growing dusk, candlelight shone through the windows. He swallowed hard, trying to picture her face in his mind, almost a vanished memory. Her upturned chin, her long ginger hair she'd comb by the fire every night before bed. He'd half hoped Luke and his wife had moved on and he wouldn't have to face them.

"Come on, Tundra. Time to pay the piper," he croaked and began pushing his way through the snow on the shady side of the hill. Within minutes, he stood at the foot of the steps, shuffling his feet and eying the front door. Collecting his courage, he mounted the steps. Behind him Tundra gave a soft whine. "Shhh." He motioned to the dog.

At the top, Eric stomped the snow from his boots, took a deep breath and rapped on the door. The tread of heavy steps approached, the door creaked open and Eric stood face-to-face with the man he'd turned his back on so many years before. Recognition sparked in Luke's eyes and his expression hardened. Eric snatched the ragged coonskin hat off his head and smoothed down shaggy hair. He tipped his head in greeting.

"Hello, Luke...Been a while."

From inside, a woman's voice called, "Who is it, Luke?"

Footsteps clicked through the house and a woman peeked around the corner. Eric clutched his hat tightly and rolled it in his hands, his mouth parched, years of memories caught up in one nervous moment.

"Claire. Good to see you."

She stopped mid-step, her eyes round. "Eric? Is that you?"

"I hope I'm not comin' at a bad time."

"No! Not at all." She tugged on Luke's sleeve and glanced up at her husband. "Aren't you going to let him in?"

Grudgingly, Luke moved back and opened the door wider. Eric stepped over the threshold and Tundra woofed an anxious bark.

"It's all right, boy," Eric called to the dog. "I'll be back." With a whine, Tundra sat down to await his master's return, still strapped in the harness. No sense unhooking him until he knew if they could stay.

The door clicked shut and Luke came around to stand in front of Eric, arms crossed, a glare on his face. Eric shifted from one foot to the other and looked into his brother's eyes.

"Luke...," his voice cracked. "After the things I said all those years back, I wouldn't blame you if you told me to leave, but before you do, just hear me out. I wouldn't have said those things, wouldn't have lost myself in a bottle if Sarah hadn't died. With her gone, I just couldn't see straight. It wasn't my fault. I hope you can understand that."

"Oh, I understand," Luke's eyes flashed. "I understand now just like I did then. Yes, Sarah died. Yes, it hurt. But that weren't no call for you to drink your purse—and our livelihood—dry."

Eric dropped his gaze to the floor, his worst fears come true. Seemed like just yesterday they had the same argument and time still had not healed the wounds carved deep by harsh words. He glanced at the blazing fire.

"I'll be headin' out tomorrow. Don't wanna bother you none." He clasped frozen hands together, not eager to leave the warmth. "All the same, it's gettin' late and cold. Mind if'n I hole up in a corner of the barn tonight?"

Claire bustled in between the two brothers, hands on her hips. "Eric, you will not be sleeping in the barn. Will he, Luke?"

Luke stepped back, grumbling under his breath, "He can rot in the field for all I care."

"Luke Webber!" Claire's eyebrows rose and her tone let the two brothers know the matter was settled. Luke scowled, his mouth clamped tight. Just then, a cough tickled the back of Eric's throat. He tried to choke it back but couldn't and he coughed until his chest ached.

"Eric, come warm yourself by the fire while I get you some hot tea." She motioned to the fireplace on the far side of the room.

Outside, voices and Tundra's low woof was followed by clomping on the porch and the door burst open. A boy of about fourteen or fifteen years old, Eric guessed, stepped in and shook snow off his bare head. Garrett. He was born the summer before Sarah left them. Wide-eyed innocence rested on the boy's freckled face, his brown hair tousled. Eric sucked in a breath. A few paces behind his nephew, came a girl, probably a year or two younger, hair tucked under a woolen scarf, her gingham dress clean and pressed. They regarded their visitor with curious gazes. The girl pulled the scarf from her hair and let it fall around her shoulders. The color of an autumn sunset, just like his Sarah's.

Claire laid a hand on her husband's arm. "Luke, why don't you introduce the children?"

Claire always knew how to smooth things out, to quiet Luke's temper. Too bad she hadn't been there in that pasture the day they had argued over the future of their claim—and Eric's behavior. He'd just wanted to be left alone in his grief.

Luke interrupted Eric's thoughts, his voice almost a growl. "Garrett, Sarah, this is Eric, your uncle."

Claire regarded her eldest, eyebrows raised. "Garrett, shake hands with your uncle."

The boy obediently stepped forward and held out a hand. "Uncle Eric," he said with a firm grip.

But Eric's thoughts were on Luke's words. Did he just say the girl's name was Sarah?

Claire stepped behind her daughter and placed her hands on the girl's shoulders. Eric's gaze fell to the floor, his eyes unwillingly to look on the young woman who reminded him so much of his own Sarah.

"Naming her Sarah was Luke's idea." Claire's voice was soft and tender.

He glanced up but Luke turned away and looked out the window at the winter snow outside. When he finally spoke, Eric strained to hear his words.

"Claire was with child when you left."

"We wanted to tell you..." Claire's voice trailed off.

Eric's gaze took in Claire's expression, her eyes red with unshed tears. "You wanted to tell me...but I wouldn't hear you out." He ran a hand over his face. "And when you needed me most to help out with the land and the herd, I ran."

A single tear traced a path down Claire's cheek and Sarah wrapped an arm around her mother.

Luke turned back around and shoved his hands in his pockets, his gaze hard. "We had to sell the herd when you left. Couldn't manage it alone. We've barely held onto the land. You shouldn't have gone."

"Pa!" Garrett spoke up from behind the oak dining table their ma had insisted they bring from Virginia. "Uncle Eric is family. Haven't you always said family needs to stick together?"

"He ain't welcome here," Luke muttered under his breath.

At that moment Eric realized the full impact of his actions and his heart ached at the pain he had caused. He gulped down his pride and nodded. "You're right. I shouldn't have come back. I just came to ask forgiveness, and then I'll be on my way. Luke, can you ever forgive me?" Eric looked into his brother's eyes, grateful for his nephew's words, yet ready to accept whatever Luke had to say.

"Pa, can't he stay?" Sarah bit her lip for a moment, forehead creased in thought. "You and ma said that maybe when we get extra money you could buy that new dress that I like so much in the Sears catalog. But what I really want is to have my Uncle Eric stay with us for the holiday. A real family gathering around the table, just like you used to have back east."

Luke's lips pressed thin and he eyed his brother in silence. Finally he nodded. The two regarded each other awkwardly at first then embraced warmly.

Woof!

Eric gestured toward the door. "That'd be Tundra. He's prob'ly cold. Mind if'n he curls up on the porch for a spell?"

Sarah's eyes lit up. "That's your dog?"

Eric nodded. "Old Tundra's been with me a few years now."

With a grin, the girl rushed to the door and peered out. "Can I pet him? He won't bite?"

A smile grew from deep within Eric to see her joyful enthusiasm. Sarah was more like her namesake than she would ever know. He shoved his hat back on his head and followed them out. Tundra lunged to his feet and barked again, tail wagging. As Eric unharnessed the dog, the animal lifted his nose in Sarah's direction and sniffed the air curiously.

"It's okay." Eric grinned at Sarah. "He won't hurt 'cha."

Sarah slowly extended her hand and let the malamute sniff the back of her fingers. Before long she was kneeling on the ground, running her hands through his soft gray and black ruff, heedless of the cold snow beneath her knees.

"He's beautiful!"

Tundra licked her face in reply and she giggled.

Garrett emerged from the house, a couple of old blankets in his arms, and handed them to his mother. Thanking him, she arranged them on the porch near the door. Sarah coaxed the dog up the stairs and the two women helped settle him onto the makeshift bed.

"You're spoilin' him." Eric's voice came out gruff but he couldn't keep from grinning under his whiskers.

"Well, he's cold," Sarah protested. "Aren't you, Tundra?" She pulled the blanket up around the dog.

Garrett leaned back against the porch railing next to his father. Seeing father and son stand side by side, the boy nearly grown, Eric realized with regret how much he had missed over the years. All because of his bull-headed stubbornness.

"Come on in, Eric," Claire urged. "And Sarah, don't stay out too long in the cold. Tundra might have a coat, but you don't."

"I won't be long," Sarah called back as the others stepped inside.

Claire directed Garrett to take Eric's coat and as she rushed back to the kitchen, she called over her shoulder, "You're just in time. Dinner's almost ready."

Eric self-consciously handed his crudely stitched beaver coat and fur cap to the boy and followed Luke into the parlor, then he had a thought. "Garrett, would you like to keep the beaver cap? I trapped and skinned it myself."

The young man's face broke into a smile. "Thanks, Uncle Eric." He put it on and it fit him perfectly.

The door opened and Sarah stepped in, blowing warm air into her cupped hands. At that moment Eric realized he didn't have a present for Sarah, but then recalled something that just might do for a young woman. He went out to the sled and rustled through the few items he'd brought down from the shanty. He pulled out a small bundle, carried it in and handed it to Sarah.

"It was your aunt's. I'm sure she'd want you to have it."

Sarah unwrapped the folds, and her face lit up with a smile Eric would recall until the preacher laid him to rest.

"It's beautiful, Uncle Eric." She gave him a quick hug and pulled the silver brush through her long ginger hair. "Mama!" she called out. "It's even better than the dress! Uncle Eric brought me a silver brush just like the one I'd given up on ever owning." Sarah rushed out to the kitchen to show Claire her new treasure.

"Come in and warm your hands." Luke motioned to Eric.

As he moved into the room, Eric saw a small pine tree in the corner decorated with red and white gingham bows and a long string of popcorn.

Eric smoothed down his whiskers. "It's still Christmas."

Luke nodded with a grin. "Yes, it is. You didn't miss it."

Eric sighed in relief and held his hands out to the glowing coals on the hearth. A couple of lanterns lit the dark corners of the room, the brightness chasing the shadows from Eric's heart. Home at last.

Joyous

A HAIKU

babe in a manger
angels on high praising God
redeemed heart joyous

A Grand Affair

Abbie leaned on the balcony railing overlooking the grand salon, toying with a knot halfway down the rope of pearls hanging from her neck. She resisted the urge to yank them off and flee to her room. She'd much rather be holed up there in comfortable clothes, sketchbook in hand.

Down below, a handful of guests chatted and nibbled on petite sandwiches from the buffet or sipped eggnog from crystal cups. Some of them were here to be seen, others because they truly were friends. The first group Abbie could do without.

The music was the best part of the evening. Edward had hardly left the piano bench since the new instrument had arrived a few weeks earlier. Abbie wanted to hear the lively, modern tunes like that new one "Charleston," but Mother had made it perfectly clear that was not appropriate for her annual Christmas Eve soirée. Christmas music only.

Abbie heard the chug of a car rolling up to the house and turned away from the guests and their mundane conversations. *Probably that Vincent fella Mumsie wants me to meet*, she thought. But Abbie had no interest in finding a beau. If she hurried, maybe she could escape before he walked in. She tugged self-consciously on the fringe of her newly bobbed hair and smoothed the brunette curl tight against her cheek. Mother had insisted on the fashionable haircut but Abbie wished she still had her hair long and tied back with an old ribbon. It was much easier that way.

The dangling beads along the hemline of her dress brushed her knees as she hurried for the curving stairs descending to the foyer below, chiding herself for not heading down earlier. The butler, Charles, crossed the marble floor and pulled open the front door, letting in the cool air of a Southern California December night and a chill ran from Abbie's bare arms all the way down to her bronze T-strap shoes.

She was halfway down the stairs when the newly arrived guests reached the arched doorway. The good news was that it wasn't Vincent. The bad news was that it was Mrs. Sorenson. The older woman shimmered in an ivory dress with a dropped waist, fur stole wrapped around her shoulders and grey curls peeking out from under her fitted cloche hat. Close behind, her husband shrugged out of his overcoat and pulled off his hat, smoothing back black hair streaked with silver.

"Your wrap, madam." Charles held out a hand.

As Mrs. Sorenson handed over her fox stole, her eye caught on her hostess's daughter. "Abbie, darling!"

Abbie reached the bottom step and the older woman rushed over and grabbed her by the hand.

"How you've grown!"

Resisting the urge to cringe, Abbie pasted a pleasant smile on her face instead. The woman said the same thing every year. Even though Abbie was eighteen, it seemed that to Mrs. Sorenson she'd always be a little girl.

"Mrs. Sorenson. It's good to see you." Abbie hoped she sounded sincere.

Her mother stepped into the entryway and Abbie breathed a sigh of relief as soon she was all but forgotten. With a final pat on the back of Abbie's hand, Mrs. Sorenson's focus moved to the lady of the house.

"Beatrice! How charming of you to invite us!" The older woman sounded as if she was pleasantly surprised to have received an invitation but Abbie knew that if the socialite hadn't, she would have been indignant.

Beatrice took Mrs. Sorenson by the arm and guided her into the grand salon to join the party already in full swing. Abbie kept her distance but followed the women into the brightly lit grand salon. Avoiding the various groups of chatting guests, Abbie skirted the edge of the room until she reached the table where Martha was serving cups of fruit punch and eggnog. The older black maid had been with them longer than Abbie could remember.

"There's my girl." She beamed a smile at Abbie. "I reckon you'd like a cup."

Abbie returned the smile. "Thank you, Martha. I'll have eggnog."

"I don't see your friend Sylvia." Martha handed the cup to Abbie. "Isn't she a' comin'?"

"No, Mumsie said she already left for San Francisco with her parents."

"Mm hm. Well, child, try to stay out of trouble then," she teased.

Cup in hand, Abbie strolled toward the tinsel-covered Christmas tree in one corner of the room. She pushed aside strands of silver tinsel, hunting for the red dragon ornament her mother had purchased for her years before.

Back then, Abbie had begged for a real dragon of her own. A rare owner might ride one in a parade or for some other special occasion but Abbie had never been allowed to own one, even when her mother hinted that perhaps some day she'd arrange for one to be brought to her when she'd completed her education. But her father had objected. "She'll not go about riding dragons and lose all hope of attracting a man!" he'd said and that was the last Abbie had hoped of owning one.

She frowned to think of the despised wizards rumored to hold the animals captive in the mountains. Dragons were thought to be intelligent but only a wizard would know for certain. They were the only ones who could understand the dragons' thoughts. And wizards were hard to find.

She stroked the horns and golden chest on the glass ornament, imagining how smooth a real dragon's scales must be. She loved the colors, the textures of all the dragon species. Abbie had tried to capture the details of some in paint but even though she'd been told she was a wonderful artist, she couldn't seem to get the colors just right.

"Abbie!"

The sound of her name brought her back to the present with a start. Abbie spun to find her mother motioning her over while standing next to a gentleman in a formal black tailcoat. The man smiled and tipped his head in Abbie's direction, his manner as proper as his starched white shirt and bow tie. But his gaze was almost hard. With one glance, Abbie felt snared as if she couldn't look away and something inside her *shifted*. Suddenly she felt transparent, as if he could lay bare her soul at will. As if she could keep no secrets from him.

The feeling passed quickly and Abbie blinked, feeling rather foolish. Even though the man appeared to be closer to her mother's age than her own, this was probably just a case of her mother trying to play matchmaker. Abbie gave a polite smile and headed their direction. Beatrice wrapped an arm around her daughter's waist and held her close.

"Blakely, this is my daughter, Abbie. Abbie, I'd like you to meet Mr. Blakely McClaren."

He took Abbie's hand. "Miss Steger, a pleasure."

"Mr. McClaren." Abbie tipped her head politely.

Beatrice opened her mouth to say something, then paused and clasped her hands together. "Oh! There's Mr. and Mrs. Estancia. I must speak with them. Please excuse me for a moment."

"We'll be fine, Mumsie. You go ahead." Abbie flashed a reassuring smile, falling back on the manners her mother had taught her from an early age. Beatrice scurried off to greet her newly arrived guests. In the awkward silence that followed, Abbie searched her mind for something to say.

"Mr. McClaren, do you come here often?" Inside, she cringed at the ridiculous question. Of course he didn't. This was her house and she would know if he did. She really wanted to ask him how he knew her mother, but couldn't think of a polite way to do so. One corner of his mouth lifted and Abbie could feel her cheeks warm in a blush.

"I come through town every now and then when I'm on the West Coast." Silence fell again and for a split second, Mr. McClaren's gaze darted to the French doors leading out to the courtyard.

"If you will excuse me. Something has come up." He grasped her fingertips with one hand and covered them with the other. "It was good to meet you, Miss Steger. Perhaps I shall see you again soon."

Before Abbie could reply, he spun about and exited through the double doors, leaving her with the polite parting words of a good hostess still on her tongue. She drifted a short distance to a buffet table where she could still see the man outside. She scooped up a small handful of salted nuts, trying to avoid the impression that she was watching him.

In the dim light shining onto the outside courtyard, Mr. McClaren passed the flickering torches set out for the smokers and headed into the darkness toward the wrought-iron gate at the edge of the courtyard. Abbie slipped a nut into her mouth and chewed slowly. The only thing beyond the gate was a stairway and then a path that ended at the gazebo. She'd spent many a long afternoon there nestled in with her sketchbook, where she could see down into the garden behind the main house.

One idea after another flew through Abbie's mind and she wondered what the man could be up to. Perhaps he only wanted fresh air. But he seemed to be moving with purpose. More intriguing was the possibility that he might be meeting someone. Maybe a lover or one of those floozies from the city.

Abbie's gaze danced over the party guests to see if anyone was watching. Mr. and Mrs. Sorenson were in a boisterous conversation near the piano, her mother was introducing the newly arrived guests to the Armstrongs, and in the far end of the room, her father sat in a brocade upholstered wingback chair, unlit cigar in hand, chuckling at another of Stan Woodrow's stories. Scattered here and there throughout the grand salon, clusters of guests laughed and talked, enjoying the Steger's generous hospitality.

Trying not to draw attention, she slipped past Mrs. Hanson, who was describing her aching knees yet again, and strolled out the French doors into the courtyard. In the back of her mind she heard her father's warnings not to become involved in other people's matters but she could either stand on the fringes of the older guests' boring conversations or discover the reason for their mysterious guest's actions. Given those choices, it was an easy decision to make. She glided past the torches and followed Mr. McClaren.

In spite of the cool night, the scent of jasmine hung in the air from the last blooms of the unusually warm season. Abbie inhaled deeply of the glorious fragrance, then instantly regretted it and knuckled the end of her nose against the tickle that had formed there. Stepping softly, she paused at the gate and craned her neck, ears attuned to the sounds of the night. Behind her, voices broke out into a chorus of "We Wish You a Merry Christmas" but Abbie was more interested in the scuff of shoes on the steps ahead. She eased the gate open and stepped into the darkness. With fingertips hovering over the trimmed hedge along the walkway, she sensed more than felt her way. On the bottom step, her shoe crunched sand against the concrete and she cringed, waiting to see if she'd given herself away. But Mr. McClaren continued up the last few steps and onto the gravel pathway above.

With a sigh of relief, Abbie crept up one step at a time. At the top, the beginnings of a sneeze tickled her nose and she pinched it shut in desperation. *Crunch.* She froze at the sound of her own footstep on gravel, then carefully sidestepped onto the narrow strip of grass that bordered the path. Ahead she heard the low murmur of voices in the gazebo and she crept toward the sound. In the dark, all she could see were dim shadows. The closest one appeared to be Mr. McClaren. As for the other, the voice was unmistakably female. Just as Abbie suspected.

Abbie crouched behind the bank of jasmine twined along a low fence and angled for a better look at his companion...and sneezed. Not just any old sneeze, but a loud, violent one that could probably be heard in the courtyard below. She clapped both hands over her mouth and nose, but too late. The two voices in the gazebo fell silent and Mr. McClaren turned his head and looked directly where Abbie was hidden.

"You can come out now, Abbie."

A blush heated her face and she sniffed, slowly moving out from behind the vine. Mr. McClaren stepped outside the gazebo and stood with feet shoulder width apart, arms crossed.

"Come, have a seat." He gestured toward a bench inside the gazebo. Abbie's heart beat with fear and her first thought was to flee back to the safety of the house but her desire to discover the identity of Mr. McClaren's companion proved too strong.

"Come along." The man gestured as if coaxing a young child. "There's someone here I want you to meet."

Abbie stepped forward into the moonlight with faltering steps.

"Come and sit, child." The soft voice inside the gazebo purred. "I won't bite."

Abbie stepped inside the structure and sat nervously on one of the wooden benches that ran around the inside perimeter and peered into the dark. Two golden cat-like eyes flashed back at her and Abbie sucked in a breath and jumped back.

"Don't be afraid," said Mr. McClaren. He clicked on a battery-powered box lantern and what Abbie saw took her breath away. It was a small dragon. Blue scales on her back faded into green on her sides, her belly a silvery white. Abbie stared in awe. She'd never been this close to one before.

"Abbie," Mr. McClaren gestured grandly toward the beautiful creature. "I'd like you to meet Jade."

The creature dipped her head and blinked languidly.

"But that's..."

The man's face crinkled in a smile. "A dragon?"

Abbie simply nodded, mouth agape, then cast a quick glance around the gazebo's interior. "But I heard voices. You were speaking with someone. A woman..."

The man raised his eyebrows. "So it's true."

Abbie's thoughts whirled in confusion. "What's true?"

Mr. McClaren slid his hands into his pockets and tipped his head, addressing the dragon. "Should I tell her or do you want to?" The dragon turned toward Abbie with knowing eyes.

A shard of fear plunged into Abbie's heart and she jumped to her feet. "You can talk to her? But if you can understand dragons, that makes you a…a…" Her mind finished the words her mouth could not. Mr. McClaren—a wizard. Abbie wondered what he would do to her now that she knew his secret. Kidnap her? Maybe spirit her away to a cave somewhere and lock her up forever?

She had to escape, to warn her parents. Abbie eyed the entrance of the gazebo but the wizard stood directly in front of the opening, eyes intently studying hers. There was slim chance she would ever be able to get past him. Deciding on another route and not caring whether she was acting lady-like or not, she scrambled for the railing. But quick as a flash of light, Mr. McClaren grabbed her shoulders and pushed her back onto the bench.

"Not so fast, Miss Steger."

Abbie struggled against his grasp, twisting and writhing to get free, her breath little more than panicked gasps. She kicked out and caught the man on the shin and he flinched but held her firmly in place.

"Abbie! Sit still."

His voice was hard and unyielding, just like his grip. Gulping for air, Abbie clenched her fists tight and regarded her captor through narrowed eyes.

"You're a wizard."

Mr. McClaren stepped back and bowed grandly. "Yes, I am."

"What are you going to do to me?"

"He's not going to hurt you, Abbie."

The dragon's voice was melodic, smooth and fluid. Abbie stared at the creature and her thoughts spun into a whirling jumble as she realized the terrible truth—she had understood every word. Twice Abbie opened her mouth to say something, but nothing came. She tried desperately to think of a logical explanation for what was happening but her thoughts kept returning to the same terrifying conclusion. Finally she squeaked out in a tiny voice, "I can understand you." The dragon slowly nodded and Abbie's shoulders sank in despair. "But that makes me a wizard too." Her voice trailed off helplessly.

McClaren's expression softened. "Not quite. But no matter what you've heard, Abbie, wizards are not monsters."

Unshed tears stung Abbie's eyes. "Please don't tell anyone, Mr.

McClaren. You won't tell, will you? If people find out, everyone will hate me."

The dragon extended her neck and nuzzled Abbie's hand. Hot breath washed over her fingertips.

"It's not what you think," Jade purred. "You might change your mind if you listen to Blakely."

"Nothing he could say would ever change my mind. Everyone knows wizards are evil."

"Don't be so hasty in your accusations." The wizard tipped his head to one side. "Your mother asked me to come speak with you."

Abbie shook her head in disbelief. "No, I don't believe you. Mumsie would never do that. Let me go!" She lunged for the entrance but Mr. McClaren grabbed her by the arms and plopped her back down on the bench. She grunted in frustration. "If you kidnap me, you'll never get away with it. Papa will never rest until he finds me."

Mr. McClaren chuckled. "I'm not going to kidnap you." He gestured toward the dragon. "You can ask Jade. I'm not holding her against her will."

Abbie studied the small dragon. Jade shifted, refolding one of her iridescent wings and Abbie's eyes traveled over her exquisite form. She noticed the coloring was uniquely different from any she had ever seen before and she couldn't help but think about the method she might use to capture the image in paint.

"Abbie, look at her. She might be small but she's a powerful, majestic animal. Much stronger than I. There's no way I could hold her here if she wanted to leave."

"But what about your magical wizard powers? Don't you use them to control her?"

Mr. McClaren grinned and shook his head. "Even if I had power like that, I would never use it to force her into anything. Jade is a beautiful, wild creature." He paused and ran a hand down her smooth scales. "And she's my friend."

Jade closed her eyes and leaned into the caress, like the kitchen cat did when Abbie stroked her back.

"You see, Abbie, the term 'wizard' is actually a misnomer. Unlike popular opinion, wizards are just like anyone else. The only difference is that we can hear dragon-speak and our association with them allows us to think on a higher level than most. When partnered with a dragon, wizards can create amazing things. That's what makes people think it's magical."

Abbie found it hard to believe his words, even though Jade did seem to be enjoying the attention. But still, it didn't make sense. "That can't be right. You're lying."

Mr. McClaren shrugged. "You don't have to believe me. But the fact exists that you have a gift. You have a rare opportunity before you. True, you can choose to refuse your wizard abilities, but…if you choose to develop them, you will find yourself in some very good company."

Abbie sniffed. "You can't prove that."

"Oh, but I can!" Mr. McClaren's eyes took on a new sparkle. "Perhaps you've heard of Albert Einstein and his general theory of relativity? His partner, the legendary Amazonian dragon, Aella, was by his side while he worked." He paused. "Or how about Hans Christian Jacobaeus?"

Abbie mutely shook her head.

He sighed. "Ah. Not a big surprise. Not many know of him outside the medical community. But regardless, his dragon partner helped him develop the cystoscope."

"The what?"

Mr. McClaren waved his hand and turned away. "Never mind. I think I've made my point. Perhaps you lack the intelligence necessary to become part of the society of dragonmasters. Maybe you don't have what it takes after all."

The remark stung and Abbie sat up indignantly. "I'm not lacking in anything!" She stared at the man, her mind full. She didn't know what to think. Mr. McClaren raised his eyebrows and waited while she collected herself. Then a thought occurred to her. "Wait, if what you say is true, what have *you* accomplished?"

"For one thing," he sat on the bench across from Abbie. "It's not about me. It's a partnership. I couldn't do much without Jade's help. For another, not all wizards are world-renowned. Some of us prefer our anonymity." He leaned back, arms folded. "Jade and I compose music—usually for other people to play."

Abbie bit the corner of her lip, her thoughts running deep. "So why are you telling me this?"

"Well," Mr. McClaren ran a hand over his chin. "You have talent—your mother said you are already an amazing artist. Combined with the fact that you can hear Jade's thoughts signifies that you have the potential to become a great wizard. If you found a dragon partner with similar interests, I'm certain your artistic talent would develop even further."

For Abbie, the words "artistic talent" put a new spin on the entire issue. If being a wizard would help her develop her skill…that would be something she might be able to buy into.

Mr. McClaren leaned forward, elbows on his knees. "Now you have a choice, Abbie. One option is to do nothing. I leave, you go back to your parents and life continues on as always." He studied her for a moment.

"But I suspect that you long for something more. You are an artist and you have a reservoir of talent deep inside that has yet to be developed. But that will never be fully realized unless you find a dragon partner and learn its ways. You can start that process by studying at one of our academies. That is your other option."

Abbie stared at him, her mind numb from so much new information. "You have an academy too?"

The wizard nodded. "We have several scattered around the world. Each one is an interesting collection of incredibly bright people. I think you would find it rather stimulating. At the academy we learn about our talents and how to care for the dragons and partner with them. Dragons come, attracted to the aura produced by so many wizards together in one place. They too seek fulfillment. Once you meet the right partner, you will both learn how best to work together."

The more she learned, the more questions Abbie had. "Is that where you and Jade met?"

Mr. McClaren nodded and Jade laid her head on his shoulder.

For the first time, Abbie considered the possibilities and what the implications would be if she actually went to the wizards' academy. But then she remembered her parents. She couldn't imagine they would ever approve such an outlandish idea. And then there another issue. Abbie crossed her arms.

"If what you say is true, why would my mother call you? She never said anything to me about this. Or about you. Why have we never met before?"

"Perhaps there's more to your mother than you realize. We were school chums years ago and we've kept in touch. She contacted me a short time ago and told me you had recently turned eighteen. And how much you love dragons. She seems to think that you have extraordinary artistic talents that could be developed even more under the right circumstances."

Abbie rubbed her arms against the increasingly cold night air. Without a word, Mr. McClaren slipped off his jacket and draped it across her shoulders. Abbie pulled it tight, grateful for the warmth. In her mind, the pieces started to fall into place. She had always loved dragons and for the first time she had someone who could answer her questions. Spurred by curiosity, Abbie began to ask one question after another. After a time, Mr. McClaren interrupted.

"We should probably go in now." He leaned to one side and peered down through the trees to the house below. "I believe all your guests have gone."

Surprised, Abbie followed his gaze and found that the house was indeed quiet. She gasped. "I didn't realize the hour! Mother will be furious."

Mr. McClaren chuckled. "I wouldn't worry. Your mother knows exactly where you are. In fact, she thought it likely you would follow me if I walked out suddenly. She also is certain you have a decision to make."

Abbie sighed. No wonder her mother had been acting so strangely ever since her birthday last month.

Hand on Abbie's elbow, Mr. McClaren guided her back to the gravel path, Jade following close behind. Abbie couldn't help but be amazed that despite the dragon's bulk, she was really quite graceful. Abbie longed to sit and talk with her more but the hour was late. She hoped she would have another chance sometime. Turning, Abbie wrapped her arms around Jade's neck.

"I hope we can talk again soon."

"As do I, Abbie."

Abbie stepped back and Jade crouched, then with a jump and mighty flap of her wings, she took to the skies and disappeared behind the treetops.

One hand on her elbow, Mr. McClaren escorted Abbie down the steps and into the house. Inside, Abbie's mother sat in a chair by the fireplace, an old leather-bound book in her lap, her father in a neighboring chair. On the hearth, small flames danced on glowing coals, radiating warmth into the room. Beatrice looked up and smiled, a sparkle in her eyes. She placed the book on the lamp table beside her.

"I see you found Mr. McClaren."

Abbie stopped, arms folded. "So you did know about this." It was more a statement than a question.

Beatrice looked to the wizard. "Well, Blakely, what do you think?"

"You were right," he said. "She has the ability."

She nodded. "I thought so."

Abbie could keep quiet no longer. "Mother, I don't understand. I thought you didn't like wizards."

Beatrice shook her head, making a dismissive gesture with her hand. "Nonsense, dear. I never said that. Mr. McClaren and I were classmates—at the dragonmasters' academy."

Abbie had thought that nothing else could surprise her that night, until her mother's revelation. She sank down onto the couch opposite her mother. "You? At the academy?"

Mr. McClaren sat in a nearby chair. "She had amazing talent as a trainer."

"Mother, what happened? Why did you leave?"

"I fell in love with your father and getting married seemed more important than finishing my training. It's a very rigorous process. I trust Mr. McClaren has explained it to you?" She looked at the man and he nodded in confirmation.

"Abbie, dear," Beatrice rose and sat next to her. "Whether or not you attend the academy is your decision. I just want you to know the truth. If you go, you may be away for years at a time and there will be times when you need to travel extensively on official business. You'll be forfeiting friends and a normal life."

"But you and Papa are happy."

Beatrice nodded. I had to make the same decision that is facing you. But I had already met the love of my life. The duties of a dragon-master proved to be too difficult for me to manage. My place was here with your father. And I'm so glad I made that decision." She brushed the back of her fingers against Abbie's cheek. "I got you instead and I wouldn't trade that for the world."

"Maybe I shouldn't go then." Abbie looked down at her hands.

"Darling," Beatrice placed a finger under Abbie's chin and drew her head back up. "I don't want you to live *my* life. I want you to live the life that's right for you. If you want to go to the academy, then you should go. I want you to have a rich life, full of wonder and excitement, not copy someone else's life that's not right for you."

Abbie turned to her father. Throughout the entire conversation he hadn't said a word.

"Papa? Why haven't you said anything?"

Adrian cleared his throat, drumming his fingers on the chair's armrests. "I will be honest with you, Abbie. I don't want you to go."

Disappointment flooded Abbie's heart. "But Papa…"

He held up a hand. "Let me talk, Abbie. I need to say this."

Abbie bit her words back and waited.

Adrian shifted in his chair, then stood and paced. "Your mother's right. Even though I do not have the ability to ever be a wizard, I know that life at the academy is rigorous and hard. When I met your mother, I could see she was a good student, but I also saw her struggle. Ultimately, it was her decision to stay or come with me. Although I loved her, I did not try to sway her one way or the other. That was a decision she alone had to make." He turned to Abbie. "As do you. You see, Abbie, I too want what's best for you. It's not easy for me to let go of you, knowing I might not see you for years at a time. But neither will I stand in your way if that is what you decide to do."

Abbie bit her lip, thinking hard on her father's words. And yet, she already knew what she wanted.

"Papa," Abbie's voice was quiet, barely more than a whisper. "I want to go."

Adrian nodded, lips pressed tight and he returned to his chair. "Somehow I thought that would be your decision. Just know that you can always change your mind and come back home to stay."

"I know, Papa. Thank you."

Abbie's mother retrieved a large, flat box from behind the Christmas tree. "Since you have made your decision already, your father and I want to give you an early Christmas present." She handed the box to Abbie.

Wondering at her parents' unusual behavior, Abbie ran cool fingertips across floral wrapping paper and removed the lid. When she saw the contents, she sucked in a deep breath. Inside, a satin evening coat with fur-trimmed collar filled the box. "It's gorgeous," she whispered. She handed Mr. McClaren his jacket and held the new coat up against her. Dolman sleeves draped down gracefully and the hem ended at mid-thigh. Appliqués of bronze Chinese dragons intertwined to form an intricate design that spread across the back and wrapped around to the front. Abbie clasped it to her chest. "I love it!"

Beatrice folded her hands in her lap and beamed a smile. "I'm so glad. I was almost certain you would end up going and the nearest wizards' academy is in Colorado. It occurred to me that a warm coat might be just the thing." After a pause, she exclaimed, "Oh! I almost forgot." She reached for the old book that had been on her lap when they came in. She handed it to Abbie. "I want you to have this. It's a book on Elementary Dragon Care. I think it will prove valuable to you over the next few years. At one time I used it quite often.

Abbie shook her head but couldn't wipe the smile from her face. "Thank you so much. I shall treasure both the coat and the book a ways."

Mr. McClaren cleared his throat. "I guess this means that you'll be joining us at the academy?"

Abbie looked at her father. "Are you sure, Papa?"

Adrian took a deep breath. "Abbie, I want what's right for you. If you want to go, I will support you."

Abbie put down the coat and book and going to her father, leaned down and kissed him on the cheek, then she gave her mother a hug.

"Well then, I should be going." Mr. McClaren rose and pulled on his coat. "Someone will contact you within the next two weeks or so."

Beatrice took his hand. "Thank you so much for coming. We appreciate your time."

Adrian shook Mr. McClaren's hand and walked him to the door.

Pulling the old leather-bound volume onto her lap, Abbie leafed through the pages. From the contents, already it was clear that she had much to learn. When her father returned, Abbie gave them each a tight hug and her parents left the room, arm in arm, to retire for the night. Abbie laid the coat on her lap and ran her hands over the silky fabric, closed her eyes and imagined dragons of all types and all sizes flying high circles in the wind and nesting down in their mountain-top aeries.

This Christmas her life had changed forever. Everything she thought she had known about wizards had been turned upside down. She set her mind to study hard in the coming year and somehow find a dragon partner to become friends with for the rest of her life, to find a way to work together and use their newfound talents to bring joy and happiness to the world around them. She would make her parents proud.

The clock chimed midnight. Christmas morning had come. Strains of a carol Edward had been playing earlier came to mind and she sang quietly to herself.

> *Enters with His blessing*
> *Into every home,*
> *Guides and guards our footsteps,*
> *As we go and come.*
>
> *All unknown, beside me,*
> *He will ever stand,*
> *And will safely lead me*
> *With His own right hand.*

With the last verse lingering in her mind, Abbie closed her eyes and drifted off to sleep. A new prayer for a new day. Life would never be the same again.

RED

The old man ran gnarled fingers through his hair and growled in frustration. His wife bustled in, wiping flour-dusted hands on her apron.

"What's the matter, dear?"

"I can't find my coat!" He leaned over to look under the bed but couldn't get past his belly. "Oof!" Every year it seemed harder to get down that far.

"Tsk, tsk," the old woman chided. "Have you been sneaking cookies again?"

"Bah!" He waved one hand in the air.

"You might want to save room so you can eat more on the road. You wouldn't want to disappoint the children."

In spite of her words, the twinkle in her eye made him smile, as always. She bustled over to the armoire and tugged open the door, then pulled out a red velvet jacket.

"Is this the one?"

One hand on each side of her head, he kissed her on the nose. "You, my dear, are amazing."

She chuckled. "But isn't the coat supposed to be in the armoire?"

"True. But even if it weren't, I'm sure you'd still know exactly where it was."

"Oh, pshaw." She waved him away but the blush in her cheeks betrayed her love. She shook out the jacket and held it up so he could slide his pudgy arms into the sleeves. She tugged the fur collar up and smoothed the fabric down across both shoulders. "Oh, don't you look handsome."

"You say that every year."

"And every year I mean it. The jacket just looks so nice on you."

"And you look beautiful in your apron with a dusting of flour on your nose." He kissed her on the cheek. The clock chimed 11:45.

"You'd better get going."

"Yes, dear. I'll be back before you know it." He gave her a wink and pulled open the door. The cold air swirled in, bringing with it a few powdery snowflakes. He called outside to his helpers, "Everything ready to go?"

A faint yell came from the barn, which he took to mean, "Yes." With a final tug on the hem of his red coat, he strode out the door toward the waiting team of reindeer. He grinned when he heard her call out behind him, "Be careful, Nick! Don't forget to let Rudolph lead. And don't eat too many cookies!"

You can find a recipe for Santa's favorite Cranberry Walnut Oatmeal Cookies in the back of the book.

A SoCal Christmas

Fall leaves and palm trees
Candy canes and snow
Presents and carols
Bright lights, lawns to mow

Hot coffee and eggnog
Pine tree tall and green
Faces are smiling
New treasures they've seen

The manger and Jesus
His love and his care
Our hearts filled with worship
His praises we bear

THE ORNAMENT

Jody walked into the living room and plopped down on the couch next to her grandfather, a napkin in her hand loaded with four chewy brownie cookies fresh from the oven. It wouldn't hurt to take a few minutes and have a snack with the old man, but her mind was already at the mall where she planned to meet her friends in an hour or so.

She offered him a brownie, and he selected one for himself with a "Thank you." With carols drifting in from the other room, they sat for a few minutes admiring the newly decorated Christmas tree.

This year Grandma had decided to go with a white and gold theme and the various patterned balls sparkled against the rich green pine needles. But right in the front, halfway up, hung an old dowel roughly the size of her little finger, suspended from a loop of common string run through a crooked hole in the top. The dowel had been crudely painted to resemble what Jody assumed was supposed to look like baby Jesus. Painted white on brown, someone had spotted a tiny face with two dots for eyes and a wide, wiggly, cheesy smile. Ever since she could remember, it had always hung in the front of Grandma and Grandpa's Christmas tree.

"Grandpa," she licked gooey chocolate from one finger, "why do you have that ornament on your tree every year?"

Grandpa chuckled. "Oh, you mean the ugly one?"

Jody grinned and nodded. She couldn't have said it better herself.

The old man took a deep breath and leaned his head back. "Well, there's a story behind that." He paused, staring at the tree. "You know your dad was in the army before he married your mother, right?"

Jody nodded.

"Well, there's more to the story that you probably don't know. I suppose you're old enough to hear it now."

Intrigued by the promise of a new story, Jody took another bite and waited for him to continue. Her friends could wait a few minutes if need be.

"As you know, your dad was shipped off to the Gulf War. He hadn't been there but a few months when a roadside bomb went off just as the vehicle he was in drove past. It flipped the Humvee over and all the guys inside got banged up real bad." He ran a hand over his face as if to wipe away the memory. "Your dad, he was injured pretty badly. They airlifted him out to Germany, where he laid in the hospital in a coma. Your Grandma and I wanted to see him, but Germany is an awfully long ways away, you know? We didn't know if he'd live and it hurt that we couldn't be there." He looked at Jody sideways with a sad smile, the cookie in his hand forgotten.

Jody had never thought about how the incident might have affected her grandparents and the thought sobered her. "So then what happened?" she asked softly.

"Well," he shifted his attention back to the tree. "Your Grandma was heartbroken. One night I was pretty upset so instead of hanging around the house and making her feel worse, I took a walk. I remember it was early December because I walked down to the park where they always have the Nativity display set up. I sat on a bench and looked at Mary, Joseph, baby Jesus, and the shepherds, and I prayed, 'Dear Jesus, please be with my son. You know I want your will to be done, but if it's possible, could you please bring him back to us?'"

His eyes glistened with unspilled tears.

"I just sat there, thinking and hoping for some kind of sign that God had heard my prayer, but God felt so far away. After about twenty minutes, a mom came by, pushing a stroller with a baby all bundled up inside and a little girl walking next to her. She was about four, maybe five years old at the very most. As they passed by, the little girl stopped and asked, 'Mister, why are you sad?' Well, I didn't know what to say. Then she held out this little ornament. 'Here,' she said. 'I made a Jesus stick at school. You can have it.' As she dropped that simple little ornament into my hand, she said, 'My mom said that Jesus is always with us. You look awfully sad so you can keep this in your pocket and Jesus can be with you too.' She and her mother continued on their way, but I knew Jesus had sent that little girl, just to remind me that he's always there for us. I took the Jesus stick home and hung it on the tree and it's been there every year since then. Just to remind us that Jesus is always here."

He wiped away a tear and Jody placed her hand over his reassuringly.

"You know, I went home and the next day we got a call that your dad had woken up. After a month or so, they flew him back to the States. He had some rehab to do, but eventually he healed up just fine."

The conversation fell silent and Jody looked again at the ugly ornament. The Jesus stick. Now that she knew the story behind it, she knew she'd never look at it the same way again. The reminder—from a babe—that Jesus would always be near.

You can find a recipe for Jody's Chewy Brownie Chocolate Chip Cookies in the back of the book.

THE PERFECT TREE

I'm gonna look over here, Mom!"

I pushed my way through a couple of close growing pine trees, neither one a good selection for the Erikson family's Christmas tree. Mom was looking for a seven- to eight-footer, perfect round and bushy. These didn't measure up, only six feet with flat sides.

I loved it up here on the mountainside Christmas tree farm. The air was clean and the pines smelled great. And now that I was fourteen, Mom had finally relented and let me go off on my own private search. In truth, though, I think part of the reason was because she had her hands full corralling the twins. At seven years old, they could be a handful and I was glad to be away from them. As I pressed on up the hill, their annoying chatter faded away.

Plucking off brown pine needles sticking to my jacket sleeve, I looked around. Up higher, it was quieter and the pines were older and thicker. Kind of like a refuge. Then one particular tree caught my eye. Maybe this was it. I started to circle around it and as I did, a rustle sounded in the brush farther on, accompanied by a slight swaying of branches. Stories of Dad's adventures hunting in the backwoods came to mind and I really, really hoped there was not a bear behind that tree. I shuddered as I got an image of me running, screaming like a girl, down the side of the mountain, dodging pine trees, a big, gnarly grizzly hot on my tail just when mom was letting me get some freedom. She'd never let me live that down.

I stopped behind one the guy had told us was a bushy Noble fir. I was ready to bolt. Then at the sound of another rustle, I froze, my pulse picking up a few extra beats per minute. *One-bu-duh-bum, two-bu-duh-bum, three-bu-duh-bum...*It felt like my heart was going to beat its way right out of my chest. It got quiet for a few seconds and I breathed easier, then took a step—only to see the branches sway again.

Surely if it was a bear, it would have shown itself by now. Maybe it was just the tree farmer?

"H-Hello? Is anyone there?" Just then the most amazing thing happened. A girl's face peeked around the edge of the tree. But not just any face. Hers was green, several shades lighter than the pine needles. When our eyes met, she pulled back, leaving nothing behind but waving tree branches.

I stood there in awe for just a moment. I wasn't good at talking to girls. But this wasn't like the girls at school. She wasn't human and she certainly didn't look dangerous. Or mean.

"Wait up!"

I started after her and when I got around the pine, all I saw were the branches of the next tree, still moving where she had passed through. I plunged after her, heading uphill, following the trail of waving branches that marked her passage. Even though I was on the high school track team, she moved so fast I started to breathe hard in the thin mountain air and even got a stitch in my side. Somewhere along the way, we left the tree farm for the older growth of the natural forest.

As I burst through a passage between two trees, I stumbled out into a clearing maybe twenty feet across. In the center grew a trio of perfectly shaped pines. The largest towered about seven or eight feet tall. My mom would love that tree in our front room. But that's as far as I got.

The girl peeked around the largest tree and slowly stepped from behind it, her hand grazing the ends of the branches. Where a normal person's hair would be, a patch of spinach green covered her head like a cap with strands falling onto her face. Spots on her cheeks shone green and lavender, shiny like the seashells the twins picked up at the beach last summer. Her ears drew back into fine points and her clothes were a lighter shade of green, little leggings, and a top tied closed with a strip of the same fabric.

"Who are you?" I whispered, afraid I'd scare her off if I talked too loudly.

"I'm Ereditha. Who are you?" Her voice was breathy but she didn't seem winded from our chase. At least she wasn't wheezing and gasping for air like I was.

"Toby. My name is Toby."

For several seconds we just stared at each other, eye to eye. I tried to think of something to say. Anything. If I kept her talking, maybe she wouldn't disappear again. After all, how many times do you get to talk to a green girl in the forest?

"Are-are you a fairy?"

"I suppose your people might think so, but my people are what would translate into your language, 'tree-tenders.'"

"A tree-tender, like in the Lord of the Rings?" As soon as I said that, I mentally slapped my forehead. She probably wouldn't have any idea what that was.

Sure enough, a puzzled look crossed her forehead. "I do not know of any tree-tenders who serve lords with rings."

"Never mind." Then I thought of the Christmas trees down the hill. "Do you prune the trees?" I had always thought the tree farmer did that.

She shook her head. "I do not. One of your kind does that work. He plants those and seems to do well by himself. He does not need our help."

"Do you tend these?" I gestured to the trio between us. As nice as the tree farmer's crops were, these were much nicer.

She nodded and nipped off the tip of one branch with her forefinger and thumb then ran her hand along the ends as if judging the straight angle by touch. "These are my favorites. I tend them often."

"They're beautiful."

She shot me the same worried look Mom had when I wrestled with the twins. "I see your people come every year and take the farmer's best trees. You will not take my trees will you?"

I shook my head and, palms out, waved my hands in denial. "No, I would never do that." At that moment, there was nothing I would do to upset her. "Does it bother you when we cut down the farmer's trees?"

"No. Those are not my trees. I only tend the trees I plant." She paused and tipped her head to one side inquisitively. "Why do you take his trees?"

"Well," I tried to think of how to say this so it would make sense. "We buy them for Christmas."

"And what do you do with them?"

"We take them home and put them in our houses."

She shrank back in surprise. "But they will die. Why do you put dying trees in your houses? Would it not be better to take them with their roots and plant them outside your house?"

I took a deep breath and looked up at the sky, trying to remember the story I had heard years ago of why we started decorating trees. "I'm not sure exactly where the custom started." But she had already moved on.

"What is this 'Christmas' you speak of?"

"It's a holiday where once a year we celebrate the birth of Jesus."

Ereditha's eyes brightened. "Oh! I have heard of this Jesus. My people say the Almighty One sent him to save your people because you disobeyed him."

I snorted. "Yeah. You could say that. But…what about you? Don't your people serve God?"

Her eyes grew wide in surprise. "Of course we do! We tend the trees for him."

"But you don't believe Christ died for your sins?" This was beginning to get very confusing.

She shrugged her shoulders. "There is no need. We never disobeyed and gave up our calling like your people did."

She had me there. I remembered the attitude I'd had that morning when Mom asked me to help her with the twins. I toed the carpet of pine needles covering the forest floor. I realized I needed to apologize and help out more.

Ereditha stepped forward and placed cool fingertips on my arm. "But there is hope for your people, right?"

I grinned a bittersweet smile and looked up into her violet eyes. "Yeah, there's hope. That's why we celebrate Jesus' birth. He promised to help us and one day things will be right again."

She nodded with a big smile. "That is good. I thought there would be hope. I know the Almighty One is gracious."

Curiosity got the best of me and I had to ask, "How do you know that?"

"He walks with us," she said rather matter-of-factly.

Whoa. What a thought. My youth pastor said last week how we just need to open up and let God in. Every now and then I had felt a sense of calm peace before, like in church during worship service, but I always thought it was because I stayed up too late the night before playing Halo and was tired. Now this sprite says she walks with him freely like Adam and Eve had? Wow.

Ereditha glanced over her shoulder. "I should go. The elders frown on those who talk to your people. They don't trust you."

"And with good reason," I agreed. I held out my hand. "Ereditha, it was a pleasure to meet you." I would take the secret of Ereditha and her people to my grave. No one would disturb them if I could help it. After all, they didn't need our help. They already had Someone to look after them.

She looked at my hand for a moment, then gently placed her smooth fingertips on mine and nodded graciously.

"And you as well, Toby. May the Almighty One be with you."

I grinned as she disappeared among the trees like a whisper. I turned back and tromped down the hill toward the tree farm, anxious to find Mom.

"Say, Mom!" I found her scolding the kids for something or other. "Let me take them for a few minutes." I grabbed their hands while she gave me an astonished smile. "You always make Christmas so special for us, and I know how much you enjoy picking the tree." While she stood there gaping, I took them to get in line for a hot cider.

And then I decided to tell them a fairy tale while we waited. That would keep them busy long enough for her to circle the best ones, and find the perfect tree.

A BEAUTIFUL SIGHT

Tara grabbed for a handhold as her feet slid out from under her on the muddy slope, wishing she'd kept her plans to go to the beach, not come on this disaster of a hike. But no, she had to feel sorry for the poor guy who had no friends and go with him on a hike.

"Come on, girl! You can do it!"

She glared up at Kai as he coaxed her on. Four more agonizing feet and she'd be able to reach his hand.

"Remind me again why I agreed to go on this hike with you." Her legs were scratched, she was covered with grimy splotches, and the smell! Ew. The air was filled with the moldy stench of the rotten tropical swamp next to the path—if this narrow rut through the jungle could even be called a path.

Kai chuckled. "Because I promised you it would be worth it."

"Can't you even tell me why?" One more lunge and Kai caught her wrist just before she landed on her face. Hand to arm, he pulled her up to the top of the mudslide.

"It's better as a surprise. Just trust me. You'll like it."

Tara puffed a breath through strands of hair that had escaped her ponytail long before. Another mosquito settled on her arm for a midday snack and she slapped at it, leaving a muddy handprint behind.

"I put on mosquito repellant!" she moaned. "Why isn't it working?"

Kai grabbed her elbow and helped her up over a large boulder. "Just a few more minutes."

Tara shuddered. As it was, she'd probably be covered in welts by the time she got back to the hotel. "How much farther do we have to go?"

"Not far. We're almost there."

"That's what you keep telling me." Tara knew she probably sounded like a whiner but she honestly didn't know how much further she could go. When she had decided to come to Hawaii the week before

Christmas with her two girlfriends and their friend Kai from church, she had been thinking more along the lines of laying in the tropical sun on the beach, sketching for her portfolio, not tromping around in a humid jungle full of bugs and mud. But when her two girlfriends wanted to go hang gliding, she decided she'd rather keep her feet on the ground. Then Kai, originally a native of the island state, offered to take her on what he promised would be an amazing hike.

Kai grinned at her sideways. "Come on. Like I said, we're almost there. Then we'll rest a while."

Tara paused, looked up the next incline and took a deep breath. "No, let's keep going. If I stop I may not get any farther."

"All right then," he said with a smile and plunged ahead.

Tara noted wryly that he didn't have any mud or scratches on him. But then again, she wasn't the triathlete that he was.

Scrambling up the next hill, Tara took one slippery step after another and tried to keep her complaints quiet, telling herself that he was right. She could do this. But one glance ahead showed Kai cresting the next hill and disappearing from sight. Again. Gamely, Tara gritted her teeth and clawed up the last few feet.

At the top, she leaned over, hands on her knees and gasped for air.

"Here we are, Tara! You made it!"

She couldn't help but smile at his congratulations. She straightened up and opened her mouth to reply, but the sight that met her eyes took her breath away. They stood on a rocky ledge overlooking the center of a dormant volcano. The sides plunged down, verdant green plant life covering every inch of ground. Here and there, white waterfalls plummeted down, disappearing into the jungle far below. Birds of red, green, blue and orange flew from tree to tree, their calls echoing through the air.

"This is amazing!" she whispered, unable to take her eyes from the incredible sight. "It's like paradise."

"Yeah." Kai's voice was low, almost reverential. "I thought you'd like it."

"How did you find this place?" Tara darted a glance his direction.

He flashed a lopsided grin and shoved his hands in his pockets. "My dad brought me years ago. We used to come up here every now and then, just the two of us. Gorgeous, isn't it?"

Tara nodded, glad she hadn't turned back. "Definitely worth it."

The two friends sat on the rock for about an hour, chatting and enjoying the incredible view. Before she knew it, the time had flown and it was getting late. Going down was still a bit slippery and difficult to negotiate but Tara made the trip with a much lighter heart. She couldn't wait to get back to her sketchbook. She knew she'd never be able to draw the scene to perfection, but what she planned to sketch would always remind her of the amazing sight. Yes, Kai was right. The difficulty, even pain, of getting up the trail was definitely well worth the prize.

FAMILY

Get in your room and stay there!" Harrison's mother stood in the living room of their broken-down apartment and pointed to the hallway. The five-year old cringed beneath the glare of her anger and turned to obey before she slapped him. Or threw something at him like last time. He slunk down the hallway to his room, which was barely large enough for the toddler-sized mattress on the floor. He huddled in the corner and clutched Max, his tattered stuffed dog.

Before long, he heard her in a mumbled phone conversation, then footsteps to the bathroom and the door slammed shut. Harrison knew that soon she would come out and go lay down somewhere like always. Maybe later she'd clean up the needles and trash.

His stomach growled but still he waited. Once she went to sleep, he'd go to the kitchen and see if there was anything to eat on the table or counter. If he was lucky, he might find some old bread and peanut butter. His mouth watered at the thought. He stretched out his legs and hoped it wouldn't be much longer. It was mid-afternoon and he hadn't eaten all day.

Knock, knock, knock.

Harrison jumped when he heard the rap on the front door.

The knocking grew louder but he dared not move yet because his mom would come out, angry at being waked up.

"Hello?" came a voice from beyond the closed door. "Is anyone there? This is the police."

After several moments of silence, Harrison heard the door crash open and he shrank farther back into the corner, Max tight to his chest.

"Hello?" A man called out and Harrison heard footsteps moving through the front room. Soon an officer walked into his room, gun drawn.

"Hey Chris! I got a kid in here!" he called out over his shoulder. He scanned the rest of the room, then put his gun away. He leaned down and peered at him, his voice gentle. "Hey there, son. Someone here called 911. Is your mom or dad here?"

He nodded slowly.

"Your mom?"

He nodded again.

"Your dad?"

He moved his head from side to side, watching the guy.

"Where is she?"

"Bathroom," he nearly whispered, hoping she wouldn't be angry with him for telling them.

"Check the bathroom," the officer called out. "Kid says his mom's in there. She must be the one who called."

Harrison heard the doorknob rattle and the other officer called out, "Hello? This is the police. Can you open the door ma'am?"

When there was no reply, Harrison heard the bathroom door crash open.

"Troy!" The call came urgently down the hallway. "Call an ambulance. Looks like an overdose."

The officer swore under his breath a word that Harrison heard his mom say when she was really mad. "Stay here, kid." He grabbed for his radio and rushed out into the hallway, talking into his shoulder.

Harrison hugged Max to his chest and pulled his legs up, making himself as small as possible.

After a bit, sirens came from outside and the ambulance people brought in big toolboxes to where his mom was. The same police officer that had talked to him before walked over and knelt down in front of Harrison.

"Hey, buddy. I'm Officer Troy. What's your name?"

"Harrison," he whispered from behind Max.

The police officer nodded. "Good name. I like it." He wiped his jaw. "How about if we go outside and get you something to eat. Would you like that?"

Harrison's tummy hurt. "I s'posed to stay here."

Officer Troy's gaze softened. "It's okay, Harrison. Your mom won't mind, she's not feeling well and we need to let the paramedics take care of her." He held out his arms. "Come on. It'll be alright."

Reluctantly, the little boy pushed himself up. With strong arms, the officer picked him up and they went outside where two police cars were parked next to the ambulance. There were lots of lights flashing over the dirt where he played sometimes when his mom felt like letting him go outside. When they reached one of the police cars, the man started to lower Harrison to the ground, but he clung tight.

"Hey, it's okay, buddy. I won't put you down if you don't want to."

Harrison pressed in close against the officer's chest, clinging onto his neck with one arm, the other clutching the threadbare dog. The officer sat in the front passenger seat of the cruiser, the boy on his lap.

"So who's this?" He nudged the dog's chin.

"Max."

"I see. Max seems like a good friend, huh?"

Harrison nodded.

Before long, another car pulled up and Officer Troy called to a lady who headed their way, her heels *click, clicking* on the pavement. When she reached them, she squatted down and put a hand on Harrison's knee.

"Who do we have here?" Her voice was gentle and her eyes kind as she looked into his face.

"This is Harrison."

"Hello, Harrison. My name is Miss Kimberly." She asked him some questions, the same ones that Officer Troy did. Harrison answered them the best he could when Max said it was okay.

"Kim," the officer addressed her. "We were just talking about getting a snack. Did you happen to bring anything with you?"

She smiled and nodded. "I have some juice and crackers in the car. Would you like some?"

Harrison was hungry but he didn't want to let go of Officer Troy, so the man carried him over to Miss Kimberly's car. He opened the passenger door and crouched down next to it.

"Come on, buddy. Why don't you have a seat here. I'll stay with you. I'm not going anywhere."

Reluctantly, Harrison let go and the officer settled him on the seat. The lady opened the trunk and brought him a box of apple juice and a bag of Goldfish crackers. She poked the straw in the box and held it out for him. After a little coaxing, he took the juice box and chanced a sip. The cold, sweet liquid filled his mouth and he swallowed, then took another sip. He'd never had any juice that tasted that good before.

Miss Kimberly opened the bag of crackers and held it out but with the juice box in one hand and Max in the other, he didn't have any free hands. Soon, however, the juice was gone and Miss Kimberly traded him the crackers for the empty box. He dug a half-dozen yellow Goldfish out of the bag and shoved them in his mouth.

"Poor little guy's half-starved," Officer Troy muttered. Just then, his radio squawked and someone asked him a question. "Hey, buddy," he said gently, "I want you to go with Miss Kimberly. She's gonna take good care of you."

Harrison stared back at the officer, the crackers in his hand almost forgotten. The officer ruffled his hair a bit but it felt nice. "I have to go now but everything's gonna be okay. Miss Kimberly is going to take care of you while your mom's at the doctor." And with that, Officer Troy was gone.

Miss Kimberly buckled Harrison in a booster seat and drove him away. She stopped pretty soon and got out. She took his hand and together they walked through the front doors of a big building. Inside stood the biggest, most beautiful Christmas tree Harrison had ever seen. It was even taller than Miss Kimberly. They never had a tree in his house but he knew some neighbors who had one once.

They took the elevator upstairs, where Miss Kimberly said she had an office, and she asked him more questions, made some phone calls and before long, they were in her car again driving across town.

It started getting dark and the lights outside were flicking on, one at a time. As they got farther from her office, Harrison saw one house after another decorated with bright strands of lights and lighted lawn decorations with trees, Santas and reindeer.

He fell asleep in the car and when he woke up, he saw that they had pulled up in front of a two-story house. Miss Kimberly parked the car and came around to open his door. She took him by the hand and headed for the sidewalk leading to the front door.

Where the yard outside his apartment was dirt, this house had a thick green lawn. Bright strings of white lights decorated the roofline and lighted wire bears stood on the lawn next to a small tree decorated in tiny red and white lights.

Harrison couldn't pry his eyes away from the lights. They were the prettiest things he had ever seen. At the front door, Miss Kimberly pushed the doorbell button with a manicured nail. Presently, a woman in jeans and a sweatshirt opened the door.

"Mrs. Adelstein, I'm Kimberly Benton, and this is Harrison."

"Yes. Please come in, we've been looking forward to meeting you, Harrison. You can call me Mrs. A."

Miss Kimberly led Harrison into the house by the hand and they followed Mrs. A. into the family room. In the corner of the room stood a Christmas tree that was more than twice as tall as he was. Underneath the tree were lots of presents wrapped in bright paper with bows and ribbons gaily decorating the top of each.

They sat on the couch and the older woman knelt on the floor in front of the little boy.

"I'm so glad you're here, Harrison."

He just stared at the woman, holding Miss Kimberly's hand tighter.

"We have a special bed just for you," she said, "and some toys you can play with. I know you're going to have fun here."

Harrison didn't answer. He looked from Mrs. A. to Miss Kimberly and back again.

"Harrison," Miss Kimberly placed a hand on his knee. "You stay here with Mrs. Adelstein. She'll take really good care of you."

Harrison waited on the couch as Miss Kimberly and Mrs. A. walked back toward the door, where they exchanged a few words in voices too quiet for him to hear. Once Miss Kimberly was gone, Mrs. A. came back in, took Harrison by the hand and led him into the kitchen, where she fixed him a bologna and cheese sandwich. He climbed up into a chair and had two bites already eaten by the time she placed a glass of milk on the table next to his plate. She sat across the table from him, her chin in one hand and watched him, smiling. She talked about some other kids who were at a church choir practice but he didn't know anything else about them.

After only a few more bites, the sandwich was gone and the milk glass empty. Mrs. A. picked up his plate and headed for the sink. Harrison placed Max on the table and laid his sleepy head on the soft fabric, arms wrapped tight around the stuffed animal.

When she finished clattering the dishes, Mrs. A. scooped him up into her arms and carried him upstairs. She helped him change into a pair of pajamas, and he tried to keep her from seeing the bruises and scrapes on his arms.

After using the restroom, Mrs. A. showed Harrison a twin-sized bed. He crawled up on it and ran his little hands over the quilt top, fingertips playing with the little yarn ties holding the quilt together. Mrs. A. pulled back the covers and tucked him in between two soft white sheets that smelled like flowers. She sat on the side of the bed and adjusted the covers.

"Did you know that Christmas is tomorrow?"

Wide-eyed, Harrison looked down at Max, the only Christmas

present he ever remembered getting. The last thing his mother had given him.

"Where's my mommy?"

"Oh, honey. Your mom was very ill."

Harrison chewed his lower lip. "Is she going to come back?"

Mrs. A. pressed her lips into a thin line. "No, Harrison. She's gone. She won't be able to come back."

"Did she die?" Once Harrison had seen one of his mom's friends shoot up with a needle and something went wrong. She died too.

Mrs. A. nodded her head without a word. Harrison clutched Max a little tighter and buried his face in the pillowy material. But he had no strength left to cry. She wrapped him up in her arms and held him, humming a little song until he fell asleep.

❄ ❄ ❄

Harrison opened his eyes to find the sun shining in the window. It took him a minute to remember where he was and then it all came rushing back. The police, the ambulance, Miss Kimberly, Mrs. Adelstein. His thoughts whirled with confusion.

But there was the most wonderful smell in the air that made his stomach grumble so he climbed down out of bed. It took him a minute to remember where the stairs were and when he got halfway down, he froze. Wrapped up in a robe, Mrs. A. sat on the couch talking with a man in his pajamas. When she saw him, she hopped up. "Good morning, Harrison!" She took him by the hand and brought him to the couch and pulled him up onto her lap. "Harrison, this is Mr. Adelstein."

The man smiled warmly. "It's very good to meet you, Harrison. And you got here just in time for Christmas!"

Harrison clutched Max tight, unsure of what to say.

"I'm sure the other kids will be up soon. Meanwhile, I think Mrs. Adelstein has cooked up something yummy for breakfast. Come on," he urged, "let's go see what she made." He held out a hand and Harrison slid one hand into his big one, and they followed Mrs. A. into the kitchen where she dished gooey, warm cinnamon rolls onto plates. He was just finishing the last couple of bites when a teenage boy walked into the kitchen.

"Do I smell cinnamon rolls?"

"Yes, you do! And Scott, I'd like you to meet Harrison."

Scott waved a hand. "Hi." He slid into a kitchen chair with a plate of the fragrant rolls. "I think Amanda's coming down too."

Mrs. A. chuckled. "What makes me think you woke her up?"

Scott grinned. "Someone had to."

"Yeah, right," Mr. Adelstein said, heading for the coffee pot. "I think you woke her up because you're excited about it being Christmas morning."

Within a few minutes, Amanda, who was smaller than Scott, came in, yawning. She smiled at Harrison too, then grabbed a roll for herself and ate it leaning back against the counter. After Harrison had finished two rolls and was starting on this third, Mr. Adelstein clapped his hands and rubbed them together.

"Who's ready for Christmas presents?"

The kids scrambled for the family room and with a big smile, Mrs. A. took Harrison's hand and followed them. Everyone found a seat except for Amanda.

Not sure what was going on, Harrison hugged Max close and pulled his knees up, sinking back into the couch as far as he could go.

"Stockings first!" Mrs. A. announced and Amanda handed one to each person. As soon as they got theirs everyone upended the stocking, the contents spilling out onto their laps. Harrison just sat and watched the commotion. Mrs. A. held a plaid one out to him.

"This one's for you," she said gently. "Don't you want to see what's inside?"

Tentatively, he reached forward with one hand and pulled the stocking onto his lap, then held the opening wide and looked inside. He reached in and pulled out a full-sized Snickers bar, his eyes wide. He'd never had one all to himself before.

"Go on," Amanda urged. "There's more."

Next Harrison pulled out a bag of gold nugget gum, a few candy canes, a chocolate Santa and a giant plastic tube shaped like a candy cane but filled with M&Ms. The little boy didn't know what to say. He'd never seen so much candy in one place before except at the store.

Once all the stockings were empty, Amanda passed out a couple of presents and then picked up a large, flat box.

"This one's for Harrison," she said with a wide smile and laid it on the couch next to him.

Harrison slowly opened the box and found a Hot Wheels track with two cars.

Scott plopped down on the floor next to him. "Let's see what'cha got there, kid."

Harrison tilted the box so the teenager could see the front.

"Whoa, that's pretty cool. Want me to help you put it together?"

Harrison nodded solemnly and before long the track was all assembled. It ran in a great oval with a loop leading to a jump right in the middle. Scott popped the two batteries into place and turned it on.

With a crooked grin, Scott held up one Hot Wheels car. "Watch this," he said, wiggling his eyebrows up and down. He placed the car on the track and as it rolled forward, the rattling gears grabbed the car and flung it down the track, where it caught speed and spun up and around the loop. One corner of Harrison's mouth twitched up in a smile and before long, he and Scott were taking turns putting the cars through their paces.

Then Mr. Adelstein opened a book and began to read a story about a lady named Mary who had a baby in a stable with animals, and angels singing to shepherds. When he had finished reading, Mr. Adelstein took one look at Harrison and asked kindly, "Have you ever heard that story before?"

"No." He shook his head.

"It's a good one, isn't it?""

Harrison nodded.

"Did you know that that little baby named Jesus grew up? He taught all kinds of people about God. He taught us how to be a family."

Harrison looked down at Max and played with one of his floppy tears.

"And you know what, Harrison?" Mrs. A. wrapped her arms around him. "That means you too. We want you to know that we're so glad you're here to celebrate Christmas with us."

Harrison looked up at Mrs. A., who wiped at a tear that fell from his eye. He looked down at Max and thought of his mother. He knew he'd never see her again. He looked up at Mr. and Mrs. A., then at Scott and Amanda.

And then he let Mrs. A. give put her arms around him and Max didn't even complain that he got squished in their hug.

❄ ❄ ❄

You can find a recipe for Mrs. Adelstein's Gooey Cinnamon Rolls with Cream Cheese Frosting in the back of the book.

THE MISS CHIEVIOUS
CHRISTMAS TREE

The first thing I noticed when I awoke was the fragrance of the Christmas tree downstairs. One of the best things about Christmas, in my opinion. Like usual, we'd purchased it the night before, the Friday night after Thanksgiving. As soon as the left-over turkey was bagged and in the fridge, Mom was always ready to jump into the Christmas spirit. The earlier, the better as far as she was concerned and that was fine with me.

That early in the morning and as quiet as the house was, I guessed Mom and Dad were still asleep, taking advantage of the long weekend. I followed my nose downstairs to where the eight-foot pine stood in the corner waiting for lights and bulbs, tall and regal as if still in the forest. A bit out of place next to our leather couch and Mom's prized Tiffany lamp.

I flopped down on the couch and leaned back, wondering if Mom was going to use the colored lights or the white ones this year. Then something caught my eye. A glimmer deep inside the tree. I tipped my head to see better. Some little kid must've stuck a candy bar wrapper or something in there so he wouldn't have to find a trashcan.

I hunched down in front of the tree and pushed aside a branch. Instantly, the glimmer dimmed. What in the world? I looked around to see if there was anything nearby I could use to fish out whatever it was. If it was a mouse or something I sure didn't want it to bite me, or worse, run up my arm. I shuddered at the thought, glad my friends couldn't see me now. This was not the type of reaction that would bol-ster the reputation of a sixteen-year-old guy like myself.

That's when I heard the musical tinkle. Wait a minute. Christmas trees aren't supposed to chime.

Curiosity roused, I grasped the tip of one branch and pulled it to one side. Sure enough. There was something in there. I breathed a

shaky sigh of relief, laughing at myself. Just a ball of that plastic webbing they use to tie up the smaller trees at the lot before they strap 'em
to the roof of your car.

I reached in and tugged but it was pretty tangled up. I pried the
offending strings away from the tree branch and pulled out the mess. I
started to ball it up and head for the trashcan when the webbing yelled
"Ow!" and wiggled in my hand. I dropped that ball of string faster than
Santa sliding down a greased chimney. I could've sworn I heard a little
grunt when it hit the floor.

So there I was, standing in my pjs, barefoot, hands in the air, staring at a twitching ball of string between my feet. Within five excru-
ciatingly long seconds, a little head about the size of my thumbnail
popped out of the tangle, followed by a little pair of shoulders. A pair
of miniature arms pried the rest of its body and legs out. It looked
human but I'd never heard of a human four inches tall. It stood up,
straightened its clothes and with a scowl, kicked the string, caught a
tiny bare foot, and tripped.

I snorted a laugh, which earned me an itty-bitty frown. I pressed
my lips together, trying to still the smile from my face.

"What are you staring at?" It tugged at its long shirt, which
reached down just above the knees.

"Well, um..." I racked my brain for something intelligent to say
but came up blank. It's not every day some little creature tumbles out
of your Christmas tree.

"What'sa matter?" It brushed off pine needles that dwarfed tiny
shoulders. "Never seen a fairy before?"

I stepped back before I tromped on the little thing. "Actually,
no, I haven't." What I really was thinking was, *This is crazy. Fairies
don't exist.*

"I know what you're thinking and, yes, we do." The fairy crossed its
arms. "And no, I can't read minds." Its voice had a musical quality, kind
of like Mom's wind chimes hanging from the back deck. "They call me
Miss Chevious, but you can call me Missy."

She continued. "Well? Aren't you going to introduce yourself?"

"Um, yeah, sure. I'm Stan." I wondered if I should try to shake her
hand, but I'd probably just squish her little fingers like Play-Doh.

About this time I'm thinking that this is the weirdest thing that'd
ever happened to me. "So, uh, how did you get in the tree?" Ok. That
was lame but it was the best I could come up with.

Missy cocked her head sideways and looked at me as if I was the stupidest person on Earth. "I flew, of course." Just then, a tiny pair of wings sprouted through slits in the back of her shirt and she flew up to hover in front of my face.

I shook my head and ran a hand over my eyes. "Oh boy, wait until Mom and Dad see this. They're never going to believe it."

"Oh! No, no, no, no!" Missy shook her head so hard, her short red hair actually ruffled. "You mustn't tell them!

Now it was my turn to put my hands on my hips. "And why not?"

Missy's little eyes welled up with tears the size of mist and she wrung her hands. "Please. I already broke Law Number One in the Fairy Rule Book."

I hate it when girls cry. It always makes me feel so helpless and they end up getting anything they want. Just like Miranda, who always gets the guys to do her dirty work in biology lab. Every day. But that's another story. All I could say was, "Ok, ok, I won't tell them." I cupped my hands in front of me and Missy settled down into them, wiping her nose with the back of one hand. I leaned down to peer into her face. "Are you ok?"

She gave a big sniff. "Other than the fact that I'm lost and," she stretched one leg out in front of her and gingerly flexed her foot, "I think I twisted my ankle." Her lip quivered like she was about to cry again.

"Do you want to sit down?"

Missy tipped her chin down and looked at me, eyebrows raised. After a second she looked at my hand underneath her and I realized she was already sitting down. Slightly embarrassed, I chuckled, then Missy tinkled a chime of a giggle. Nothing like laughter to lighten the mood. A bit more relaxed, I sat on the couch and carefully lowered her to the armrest.

"So what do we do now?" I asked her. "You don't know how to get home and I can't tell anyone."

"Oh, I know how to get home. I just don't know where I am." She nodded her head briskly. "All I have to do is to fix something—you know, make it perfect—and a portal will open up for me."

Now I was really confused. As if it wasn't enough to find a fairy in my Christmas tree, now I was supposed to help her make something perfect? "How do you do that?"

"I don't know." She waved dismissively with her hand. "You just do."

"So how about if I break something so you can fix it?"

She shook her head. "No, it doesn't work like that."

"O...k..." I'd have to think about that one for a while. "So what is this Fairy Law Number One that you've broken?"

Missy sighed deeply, shoulders slumped. "Never let a human see you."

"Meaning me."

She nodded.

I didn't mention that she looked a bit embarrassed. She was a screw-up, and I knew how she felt.

I heard the creak of the floor upstairs. Someone was getting up. "Missy! Someone's coming...we have to hide you!"

Her face brightened. "You don't have to do that. I can be invisible to whoever I want to be invisible to."

"Then why did I see you?"

Her voice was so quiet I could barely hear. "I was stuck and needed help."

The shuffle of Mom's Tweety Bird slippers sounded down the stairs. I clamped my mouth shut, afraid she'd hear us talking. Mom appeared around the corner, running her fingers through mussed-up, bed-head hair.

"You up already?" She stifled a yawn and headed for the kitchen. "Did you fix the broken lights for me?"

Oops. "No, not yet."

Mom tipped her head and glared through sleepy eyes. "Honey..."

"I know, Mom. I'll get to it soon." I hoped she wasn't going to ask about the history class project I was supposed to finish before Christmas break. Hadn't gotten to that yet either. My grade was riding on that project and she wouldn't be happy with me if she knew. Thankfully, she didn't ask.

She sighed and continued on her way. "Hungry?"

I was, of course, but now that I was a fairy-sitter, I didn't know what to do. Do I eat or do I find somewhere to hide her first? Missy stood up and gestured grandly with one little hand as if inviting me to the kitchen, kind of like Vanna White displaying the next puzzle on Wheel of Fortune.

I couldn't help but roll my eyes. "Yeah, sure, Mom. Coming." It felt weird leaving the fairy behind but there was nothing to do about it. I scooped up the ball of plastic twine and headed for the kitchen. But no sooner had I turned my back on Missy, a missile zoomed past my head, parting my hair as it flew by. I ducked and covered my head with one hand, then looked up to find Missy sitting on the edge of the kitchen island, swinging her feet over the edge. Mom was looking at me with one eyebrow raised.

"Are you ok?"

"He he," I tried to chuckle. "Felt like there was something in my hair." I brushed at it. "But I guess nothing's there." I dropped the twine in the trashcan.

Without a word, Mom returned to rummaging through the refrigerator. Her voice came muffled from deep within, somewhere I'd probably never go. I was afraid of what I'd find back there in the refrigerated Netherworld. "Looks like we're out of milk. Want some toast?"

I agreed and as she placed bread in the toaster and went back in to troll for some butter, I took a seat on one of the two barstools. Missy jumped up and skipped across the counter with abandon. I tried to ignore her antics but I'm not sure I was doing very well.

"Are you sure you're ok?" Mom snagged me with that piercing stare she used when I'd been playing basketball instead of doing my chores.

"Yeah, really, I'm fine." I buried my face in my hands, scrubbing at my eyes with the heels of my palms. At least that way I wouldn't have to pretend I couldn't see the fairy doing back flips over the butter dish. I heard the toast pop up and sneaked a peek to find Mom's back to me. I gritted my teeth and glared at Missy, putting as much force into my expression as possible, willing her to behave herself. But maybe I tried too hard. The joyful fairy stopped in her tracks, shoulders wilted, a sad pout on her face. Oh great. Now I felt guilty. Just before Mom turned around, I mouthed, "Sorry," and was rewarded with an apologetic little fairy grin.

Mom pushed a plate of buttered toast across to me, then took a bite of her own. "Hm…needs honey," she mumbled and went back to the cupboard.

As soon as she turned around, Missy spied the bread on Mom's plate, a half-circle bitten from the corner. Her face brightened and she clapped little hands together, producing the sound of a tiny bell. In an instant, the toast was perfectly shaped as if it had never been bitten.

Mom returned with the honey bear squeeze bottle and, hand poised over the bread, stopped and stared. I pushed crumbs around my plate with my toast and waited for the inevitable reaction.

"That's weird," she breathed. "I know I took a bite but..." Her voice just trailed off into the ether and I was happy to let it go. I dared a glance sideways at Missy and found her standing stock still, a horrified expression on her face, both hands over her mouth. Since no portal opened to take her home, I guessed that raising an unsuspecting person's curiosity wasn't exactly the way a fairy was supposed to accomplish her task. Maybe that was Rule Number Two. Don't get caught.

I shoved the remaining toast into my mouth, carried the plate to the sink and thanked Mom.

"No problem, kiddo," she said, reaching for the coffee canister.

I headed upstairs, Missy balanced on my shoulder, hanging onto the collar of my t-shirt with one hand. Once in my room, she fluttered down to the desk, sat cross-legged and bit a tiny piece off of a crumb she had picked up off the counter. I settled onto my bed and took a deep breath, wondering if my life would ever be normal again.

Missy gestured toward the door. "I saw downstairs that you have a deer that's missing its body. I could fix *that*."

I held up my hand as if motioning for an approaching semi-truck to stop. "Oh no you don't. Bad idea." Clearly she was talking about the deer head my dad had taxidermied and mounted on the wall after his Colorado hunt. When Missy tipped her head sideways curiously, I added, "That doesn't need fixing. It's exactly like it's supposed to be."

Missy looked at me as if to say, *I don't get it*, so I added, "Trust me." She shrugged her shoulders and resumed breakfast, popping the last tidbit into her mouth. She brushed off her hands and cast her gaze around my room, settling on my F-22 Raptor model plane suspended from the ceiling. Uh oh. That gaze looked like trouble. Time to run some interference.

"So, Missy..." I waited until she turned her head back in my direction. "What do you fairies do out in, uh, Fairyland."

She puffed through her bangs. "It's not Fairyland. We live in a forest. And we fix things."

"Fix things? Like what?" I couldn't imagine anything in the forest that would need fixing.

"Oh, you know, flowers, trees, stuff like that. If they break, we fix them."

"And animals too, I suppose," I said, thinking of the mounted deer head downstairs and how close we came to having a live deer prancing around the living room.

Missy nodded her head. "Sometimes."

"Hmph." I pushed yesterday's shirt off my bed onto the floor. "So what else do fairies do?"

"We play, make music." Her eyes brightened and she seemed to glow just a tiny bit. "Sometimes we have the most marvelous parties." Somehow I didn't find that hard to believe. As I sat there imagining little glowing fairies cavorting about the forest, I noticed Missy's eyes took on a far-away look, shoulders relaxed, suddenly looking very tired. Hm. A sleepy fairy could be a good thing. I looked around for something that might serve as a cozy nest and spied my NHRA ball cap, the one I got when Dad and I went to the Winter National Drag Races in Pomona last year. I snatched the cap off my bookshelf, turned it upside down and layered in a couple of socks. I made sure they were the clean ones. Missy watched with quiet interest.

I set the cap on the desk. "Here's a bed if you're sleepy." Missy gave me the warmest, sleepiest smile, then crawled over the brim and snuggled down into the socks. Kind of reminded me of my friend Enrique's puppy when it would crawl into its blankets and fall asleep. One tinkly sigh and she was out.

I stole silently across the room and eased down onto my bed, picking up *Fahrenheit 451*, the Ray Bradbury novel my English teacher had assigned to the class. I opened the book and read a couple of pages but I must have fallen asleep. Next thing I knew, I woke up with the book facedown on my chest. Missy was perched on the spine watching me, chin in hand. I shifted slowly, trying not to knock her from her precarious perch.

"Um, hi?" It's an odd feeling to wake up and find a fairy staring at you.

"You're the nicest human I've ever met," she sighed.

"Aren't I the only human you've ever met?"

"Well, yes, but I've *seen* others." Her musical voice took on an indignant quality.

This was one of those times it was probably best to not say anything at all. I excused myself, grabbed my jeans and a mostly clean t-shirt and headed for the bathroom. Once dressed, I headed down to the garage and was just fishing out my basketball when I heard my dad's voice.

"Stan, there you are. You didn't forget about the lawn, did you? We need to get it trimmed down so we can put out the Christmas decorations."

I grimaced inside. Yeah, I'd forgotten. "I'm on my way," I called back, reluctantly returning my basketball back to the shelf and heading for the lawnmower instead. I wrested the machine out of its cubby next to the workbench and rolled it out onto the driveway to check the gas and oil levels.

That's then I heard the horrendous squeal of tires on the pavement and looked up to see Mr. Beaulieu's car jerk to a stop in front of our house. Lying under the front bumper was Snowflake, Mrs. Ferguson's little Bichon Frise. I dropped the mower's dipstick on the driveway and sprinted toward the accident, knowing how much that little dog meant to the old lady. She'd be heartbroken if anything happened to him.

I reached the scene just as Mr. Beaulieu came scrambling out of his car, horror written on his face.

"He just ran out in front of me. I couldn't stop."

I nodded, certain he was telling the truth. Snowflake didn't escape often, but when he did, he could run fast as a top fuel dragster. I knelt on the ground and wrapped my arms around the little dog, who whimpered as I gently slid him out from under the car. I carried Snowflake over to the curb and sat down, cradling him in my lap. Within seconds, Missy came streaking from the house like a shooting star, hovered over us for just a second and then gently settled down onto the Bichon's furry shoulder. Stroking his neck, she crooned a sweet melody that would have put me to sleep had I not been so worried about the dog. Snowflake's head in my hand, he squeaked a little whine and I could swear he was watching Missy out of the corner of his eye. Then I felt him sigh and fall limp. My heart sank.

"No, come on, boy," I coaxed. "It's gonna be ok. Come on." What I was thinking was *Don't die*. Mr. Beaulieu shifted nervously from one foot to the other.

"Shhh." Missy continued to stroke the little dog and hum in a soft, musical purr. After about a minute, Snowflake lifted his head, turned his nose toward Missy and gave her the softest little doggy kiss. Her face broke into a warm smile and she wrapped her arms around the little muzzle, giving it a kiss in return. Suddenly I realized this is what fairies were made for. *We fix things.* Now it made sense. She had a very important job.

Snowflake struggled to sit up and licked the bottom of my chin. I couldn't help but chuckle. Trying not to let Mr. Beaulieu see, I whispered to Missy, "You fixed him, didn't you?"

Missy beamed. "It's what I do!"

"Well, you did a great job." I would have given her a hug right there if I hadn't thought I'd hurt her. Not to mention the fact that Mr. Beaulieu would've thought I'd lost my mind.

About that time, my dad came around the corner of the house with a box from the shed. "What's going on?" He spotted the car in the middle of the road, driver's door open, then me sitting on the curb, Snowflake in my lap. He practically threw the box on the ground and within seconds was at my elbow. "What happened? Is he ok?"

"The little dog," Mr. Beaulieu wrung in his hands the black beret he always wore. "He ran out in front of my car..."

Dad eyed Snowflake, who looked up, panting. "Well," he whooshed a relieved sigh and ruffled the dog's ears. "He doesn't seem too worse for the wear. Do you, boy?" Snowflake woofed in response and with a chuckle, Dad returned to the box of decorations. Crisis over.

"Come on, boy." I stood up, the little white dog tight in my arms. "Dad, I'm taking Snowflake back to Mrs. Ferguson," I called out over my shoulder. Missy perched on the back of the dog's neck as if riding an elephant, hand clutching his collar.

"Wait," Mr. Beaulieu rushed to his car. "Let me move my car and I will come with you."

Soon he and I were walking side-by-side six houses down to Mrs. Ferguson's. Face still pale, Mr. Beaulieu kept glancing sideways at Snowflake.

"You think he's ok?"

I grinned. "Yeah, I think he'll be fine." We stepped up onto the porch and Mr. Beaulieu pushed the doorbell button, then continued strangling his hat. Soon the door creaked open. Mrs. Ferguson stood hunched over as always, white hair curled and sprayed, thick glasses perched halfway down her nose. She pushed them up with one finger and peered at us. When he saw her, Snowflake struggled to get down. Missy buzzed up into the air away from the bucking bronco of a dog as I lowered him to the ground. He pranced to his mistress and danced circles around her feet, then pointed his nose up toward Missy and yipped. She pressed both hands to her mouth and blew him kisses.

Meanwhile, Mr. Beaulieu was explaining what happened, telling Mrs. Ferguson how sorry he was and that if Snowflake developed any problems to please call him and he'd pay the vet bills. Mrs. Ferguson shuffled out onto her porch and eased down into the old-fashioned cane-backed rocker she always kept there. Snowflake launched himself into her lap and wiggled excitedly.

"I don't know how he got out," she said. "But thank you so much for bringing him home. I don't know what I'd do without him." Her voice cracked and she wiped a tear. "If I don't get another Christmas present all season, this would be fine. Having Snowflake home safe is the most perfect present I could hope for."

I glanced at Missy out of the corner of my eye and shook my head. She'd done it.

Mr. Beaulieu and I said our goodbyes and he returned to his car, then drove away very slowly. I stood by the curb and leaned back against the pine tree growing between the sidewalk and street, Missy resting on my shoulder.

"I need to go," she chimed.

I nodded. I hadn't known Missy long but I already knew I'd miss her.

"Thank you for rescuing me."

"Thank you for saving Snowflake."

"Like I said, it's what we do." Her words came out matter of factly, but I could tell from her grin that's what she lived for. What she was made for. Here was a little creature who took her work very seriously.

A disk-shaped glimmer appeared in the air a few feet in front of us and opened into a small gateway the size of my hand. The portal.

Missy hovered in front of me, one tiny hand on each of my cheeks, and placed a soft kiss on the end of my nose. It tingled all warm and fuzzy-like. With one last smile, she turned and buzzed to the gateway, stopping at the entrance. One hand on the edge of the portal, she looked over her shoulder for three or four seconds, smiled warmly, then she was gone and the portal winked out.

I stood there for a moment and looked up the driveway to where the mower waited. Missy's words came to mind. *It's what I do.* If she could take her job so seriously, maybe I should too. And between the chores and my homework, I had quite a bit of catching up to do. Might as well start with the lawn.

I rubbed the tip of my nose, the magic from Missy's kiss already fading and thought about how glad I was to have met her. "I'll bet Fairyland is quite a place," I whispered to myself.

I could have sworn I heard a tinkle in reply.

"Yes, it is."

CHRISTMAS LIGHTS

A LIMERICK

There once was a man hanging lights
For to brighten and cheer the cold nights
But the lights, they fell down
And the man, he did frown
Saying, "Gah! I don't mind those cold nights."

THE GOLD MINER'S STOCKINGS

Jedediah wiggled his toes and the biggest one poked through the hole in the end of his stocking. He sighed with a frown. Once the snow thawed a bit and he could make the trek into town, he'd have to look for a new pair.

Some of the gold miners didn't care about their socks. But Jedediah did. He might not live in the city anymore, but that didn't mean he had to live like a rat in a dark hole. No, even though he lived alone, he'd built a snug little cabin, kept it tidy and his clothes in as good shape as possible.

He peeled off the dirty socks and put on his other pair, then shoved his feet into bear-fur slippers. At the little table in the corner, he poured a cupful of water into a pan and dunked his dirty socks, lathered them up with lye soap, then rinsed and squeezed them out.

When he'd built his granite fireplace, he'd included a bench-like ledge in front of the fire pit, a nice place to sit when it was cold—and a nice place to dry wet laundry in the winter. He laid the socks out on the warm stone and lowered his aching old bones into the oak rocker, pulling a tanned bearskin blanket tight around his shoulders. Christmas Eve and here he was, alone again. He rocked slowly, his mind traveling back to when he was a boy.

Christmas Eves were not spent alone then. It'd been just his mother, father and himself, but they were a happy family. Mother always baked a ham and there were presents and stockings—without holes—that magically appeared full of wonderful treasures on Christmas morning. He chuckled. Father always denied filling them but now that Jedediah was older, he knew better. But still, he was grateful that his parents had kept the magic alive all those years.

The old miner rocked long into the night, his mind filled with so many wonderful Christmases past, all of them comforting memories. At the same time, he had no regrets. After his parents died, he'd come out West to seek his fortune and in a way he had found it. He wasn't rich, but life here in the beautiful mountains lived on his own terms was enough. He knew that many people lived with far less and he was grateful for what he had.

Much later, Jedediah opened his eyes to find Christmas morning sunshine peeking through the glass window. Hadn't meant to sleep in the chair all night. He stretched and yawned, a deep breath filling his lungs with the scent of pine from the branches he'd carefully arranged on the table.

Then his eyes caught on the old stockings on the mantle. Except they weren't old anymore. The holes were gone, the yarn soft and new. They even looked a bit stretched out. He reached forward to pick one up, but then almost dropped it in surprise. It was heavy.

He sat down and dumped the contents into his lap. Peppermint sticks and pecans—his favorites. His eyes welled up with tears and he shook his head, looking toward the window. Maybe his father had told the truth and he hadn't filled those stockings every year. He'd never know the answer to that one but one thing was certain. Jedediah planned on washing his socks and placing them on the mantle next Christmas Eve, and every year after that for as long as he had socks and feet to wear them.

Teacups and Traditions

Leora put a hand on the rough wooden door of The Tipping Tea-cup and gave a push. Overhead, a brass bell jingled a greeting and the delicious scent of rosehips and peppermint transported her home where even now her mother might be settled in a favorite chair, warm cup of tea in hand.

Stepping inside, Leona's gaze ran around the tourist shop and stopped on a shelf of decorative teacups. A sign to one side read, "Clearance!" She crossed the room and scanned the shelf, then reached for a light green one rimmed in gold, maroon roses on the sides. She peeked underneath and almost gasped to see the price marked down from $34.99 to $5.95. She smiled to see the stamp on the bottom. Royal Doulton. Her sis would love it and at that price, it fit her budget perfectly. Her sister might even use it for their traditional Christmas tea.

Leora carried the cup and saucer to the sales counter, where a 20-something girl in a floral dress met her. A tiny diamond stud sparkled on one side of her petite nose and her sun-kissed auburn hair and deep tan spoke of many hours spent in the San Diego sunshine.

"Did you find everything okay?" Her smile, warm and genuine, immediately put Leora at ease.

"Yes, thank you." Leora dug in her worn shoulder bag until her fingers finally located her wallet, the purple one Grandmother had given her years ago. She paid for her purchase and watched the clerk wrap the delicate cup in tissue paper and place it inside a red plastic bag emblazoned with the store's name. She handed the bag to Leora and smiled, a playful dimple marking her cheek. "Have a nice day! And Merry Christmas!"

"Thank you…and Merry Christmas to you too." Leora hoped she sounded cheerier than she felt. She took the bag and headed out the door, the bell chiming as she left. Outside, she stepped off the rustic wooden porch and looked up one side of Old Town's pedestrian-only street and down the other. Festive wreaths hung from every lamppost, holiday decorations draping every shop. In years past, the scene had fit her mood perfectly, but this year she struggled to muster even an ounce of Christmas spirit. In an effort to remedy that, she had decided that if any place could put her in a holiday mood, it'd be Old Town and maybe she could even pick up a few gifts while there.

But now that she was here, all she wanted to do was go home. Not to the apartment where she lived, but home to her family up on the Central Coast. Soon. She'd be there now if it wasn't for her job at The Java Bar.

Ding!

Leora dug her phone out of a back pocket and peered at the screen to see a text from Mom with a picture of a Christmas tree, decorated and standing in the front room.

Got the tree up. Can't wait to see you!

She took a deep breath. The last Christmas tree in this house and she hadn't even been able to help decorate it. She shoved the phone back into her pocket and remembered all the years she and her mom had put up the holiday decorations together.

She knit her eyebrows together in a frown. Why did her parents have to sell her childhood home? She pictured Grandmother sitting in her favorite rocker by the fireplace, tapping her fingertips to the cadence of a carol. But now she was gone and Leona wondered if there would even be room in her parents' new, smaller house for the old rocker.

She turned toward the parking lot and was just passing a group of carolers singing "Silver Bells" when her attention was drawn to the old church at the end of the street. The bell tower's blue dome of the historic Church of the Immaculate Conception glinted softly in the late afternoon sunshine and something pulled at Leora, tugging her onward. Soon she found herself climbing the three red-tiled front steps. With a tug, she pulled open one of the heavy wooden doors and stepped into a hushed holy silence. A sense of calm wrapped around her like a warm down comforter.

She sank onto a back pew and leaned forward, resting her arms on the bench in front of her. Her eyes adjusted to the dim light and she studied each one of the Stations of the Cross. She didn't know much about the Catholic Church, but their traditions and beautiful build-ings intrigued her. The quiet, the ceremony, the formality awed her. While she loved her own church with its upbeat worship band, something about the old churches soothed her. She knew that no matter which Catholic church one visited, they could always expect the same. Wherever a Catholic traveled in the world they could be at home.

On religious holidays, a friend of hers back East often posted online pictures of Mass at his church. She always enlarged the photos to see the vestments, the processions, the decorations. If only she could hear the music and smell the incense. It must be an awesome experience.

But here in the quiet, sunlight eased into the nave through stained glass windows, illuminating the light blue fresco behind the altar with cherubs honoring the crucifix between them. Just in front of the altar stood two lush green Christmas trees, one on each side, the lights still dark, awaiting Christmas Eve Mass. Between the trees stood an empty manger, a beatific Mary and Joseph awaiting the holy Baby to be placed inside, love radiating from their faces.

She wondered what Christmas Eve Mass would be like in the old adobe church. No doubt hushed, calm, respectful, sacred—very different from her church. And yet a whisper inside reminded her that some things were the same. Both churches celebrated Christmas with fragrant pines, manger scenes, and most importantly, worship of the Christ child. She leaned back and clasped her hands together. That's really what it was all about. Not the shopping, the baking, the decorating or even the annual Christmas tea with her mother and sisters. Remembering the miracle of Christ's birth would always be enough. No matter where her family celebrated Christmas, they would always have each other.

Directing her thoughts heavenward, Leora mouthed a silent thank you and smiled. Nestling the red bag with the precious teacup in the crook of her arm, she stole out of the church and into the golden glow of early evening, the birds twittering their farewell to the day. Now, in celebration of God's generous gift to mankind, Leora looked forward to purchasing gifts for her friends and family. On a college student's income, she couldn't afford much but no matter how small the gift, for her it would represent God's gift to man. It comforted her to know that the spirit of the Christ-child—the true spirit of Christmas—was with her no matter where she went.

She headed for her car, a bounce in her step, ready to share the new joy she felt with everyone she met. With a grin, she pulled out her phone and texted her mom back.

Looking forward to it! Be there soon.

SILENT NIGHT

A belard Muench tugged the front of his hood down against the cold German morning and frowned, thinking back to Christmas Eve the year before—and the children. The Living Nativity was the choirmaster's crowning achievement of the year. While he loved the children and was a favorite of theirs in return, the beautiful Christmas Eve mass was always disrupted by the little ones who found it hard to be quiet and still, especially so late at night.

He had been trying to think of a solution to this dilemma for days and now he was running out of time. Christmas Eve was only two weeks away. The portly man shivered and tucked his hands into the sleeves of his brown monk's robe.

"Guten morgen, Herr Muench."

The monk gave a quick nod to the glassmaker as he hurried by, anxious to get out of the early morning cold. No sooner had he passed the merchant, however, the shop next door caught his eye. The candy maker. Of course! He pushed open the door to the little shop and let himself in.

"Guten morgen." The confectioner beamed. "What brings you into my shop this morning?"

"Candy," the monk replied with a crooked grin.

"Ja?"

Abelard explained his plan to the shopkeeper, who assured him that he could make the candy exactly like the monk wanted and would bring a bagful to him later that week. The holy man left the shop with a smile on his face. Surely this would solve his problem.

In his chambers, Abelard donned his choirmaster robes in anticipation of Christmas Eve mass. On his way out the door, he scooped up the bag of sweets left by the candy maker. He crossed himself and breathed a quick prayer, hoping his plan would work.

Once the volunteers playing the Virgin Mary, Joseph, the shepherds and the others were in place, the time came for the choir to file in. While they were moving into place, Abelard turned to the congregation and called all the children forward. As he greeted them, he held up one of the candy sticks.

Immediately, every little eye focused on him and the candy.

"Do you know what this is?" he kindly asked them.

One little girl about four years old twirled blond hair around one finger and answered in a near whisper, "Candy?"

"Ja!" He nodded his head. "It is a candy stick. Do you see the white and red stripes wrapping around it?"

The children nodded solemnly.

"Do you know what the white stands for?"

The children all shook their heads in unison.

"The white stands for the sinless life our Savior led. As the Son of God, Jesus' heart was pure and free from sin."

The children continued to stare at the candy as if it would disappear.

"Do you see the crook on the top end of the stick? That is to remind you of the shepherds." He gestured toward two men in rough robes standing next to a wooly lamb. "They came to see baby Jesus the night he was born."

He looked at the children with a big smile. "I want each one of you to have one of these candy canes to help you remember the story of Jesus' birth."

Abelard passed out the candy sticks to the children, placing a hand on the head of each one and blessing them. After all the children had been served and returned to their parents, the monk turned to the choir. Taking his place in front of the singers, he raised his arms for the first note, then paused and smiled.

Behind him, the only sounds were of the children, happily sucking on their clever treats. As he led the choir in their first song, he couldn't stop smiling, thinking about the candymaker's sticks and how these children would remember this sweetest Christmas Eve the rest of their lives.

✳ ❈ ✳

Author's Note: My tale "Silent Night" is based on a historical account of an unnamed choirmaster in 1670 at the Cologne Cathedral in Germany who bent sugar-sticks into canes to represent a shepherd's staff. The candy canes were handed out to children during the lengthy nativity services. This tradition spread throughout Europe and later to America. I have taken the liberty of adding the red stripes in my story, although there is some debate as to when the first red and white candy cane was made. Historians will note that probably did not occur until at least the mid-1800s.

TREE TOPPER

Mommy, will Daddy be back for Christmas?"

"No, honey."

"Why not?"

The little girl's brown eyes opened wide as she waited expectantly for an answer. How was Trish to explain to little Emmy how her Daddy died? She had tried before, but at four years old, Emmy couldn't completely understand the concept of cancer stealing someone's life away, bit by bit.

"Because Daddy's in heaven with Jesus, little one."

Trish wiped away a tear trickling down her face. It had been less than a year and the wounds were still so fresh. So deep. "He won't be back, baby."

Emmy climbed up into her mother's lap. "Don't cry, Mommy." She patted Trish on the cheek with soft little fingers.

Trish wrapped her arms around Emmy and held her tight, breathing in the soft, pleasant smell that was her daughter. It was just the two of them now. After a minute or so, Trish kissed the top of Emmy's head. The little girl looked up, eyes searching her mother's like she always did when a question was forming in her mind.

"Mommy, what's it like in heaven?"

The little girl's question brought to mind an image of her husband Jim walking through the gardens of heaven, singing in his beautiful tenor voice. She could feel the corners of her mouth turn up in a bittersweet half-smile. She opened her mouth to answer, but Emmy continued.

"Are there angels in heaven? With Daddy?"

Trish nodded. "Yes, honey. There are."

"Do they sing together?"

"Probably. I believe the angels sing beautiful songs. Like the one they sang when Jesus was born."

She looked at their little four-foot Christmas tree, all she cared to put up on this first year alone. The white lights on the tree reflected off the red glass ornaments and glimmered down softly onto the simple Nativity scene at the base of the tree. Mary, Joseph, and baby Jesus under a little open-sided stable. She was glad Emmy had begged for at least a small one.

The four-year-old followed her mother's gaze to the crèche. "Mommy, if the angels were there with baby Jesus, why don't we have one with our baby Jesus?"

Trish smiled and shook her head. So many questions. "I couldn't find the angel, honey." She didn't want to admit she didn't have the heart to open all the boxes. Not this year.

Suddenly Emmy's eyes lit up and she scrambled down from her mother's lap and ran to her backpack laying in the chair, dumped there after preschool yesterday. Emmy wrested the zipper open and reached inside, pulling out a paper angel with a skirt that may have once been cone-shaped.

"Look what I made, Mommy! Now we have an angel!"

Trish brushed silky brown strands of hair out of Emmy's sparkling eyes. "It's beautiful, Emmy! You did a very nice job."

Emmy's eyes shone with the praise. "Can we put it on the tree? It can look down over baby Jesus and we can pretend it's singing."

Trish nodded. "That's a wonderful idea." She reshaped the angel's skirt and positioned it carefully on top of the tree. "It's perfect."

Emmy bounced on the balls of her feet and clapped her hands. "Now we have an angel to sing with, just like Daddy."

With fresh tears misting over her vision, Trish scooped up her daughter and held her tight.

"Yes, we do, baby. Yes we do."

Peace

A VIGNETTE

Whoa there," Hank crooned to the big buckskin and slowed to a stop. Leather creaking, he leaned back in the saddle and lifted the brim of his hat, neck craning up at the dark night sky. With no moon, the stars sparkled and shone, pinpricks of light against a midnight blue canvas. The cold air threatened to creep inside his coat and he snugged the collar a bit tighter. Off in the darkness, a steer sounded a minor complaint, followed by a slight shuffle as the cattle readjusted positions, huddling close in the frigid night air.

Hank took a deep breath, inhaling the dusty, earthy cattle smell and exhaled in contentment. The plaintive sound of a harmonica drifted across the herd as old Brody played a slow refrain of "Silent Night" by the campfire. A man couldn't ask for a better life. Out here under the stars. In the peaceful quiet of a Christmas night.

WRAPPING PAPER

A POEM

Brightly colored wrapping paper
Covers boxes big and small
Some clever little packages
That aren't quite square at all.

Pretty pictures cover some
Others, light and playful scenes
While some are peaceful, calm
Angels joyous yet serene.

Through images or words
They speak of Jesus' birth
They show the miracle
Of God come to us on Earth.

But under all the paper
We wonder what's inside
Candy, toys, gadgets, clothes?
Or a humble gift to prize?

At the end of Christmas day
When all the paper's ripped and torn
I hope the joy the gifts have brought
Reflect the One who's born.

My wish for you:
May Christmas find you happy and whole,
With family and ones you hold dear.

RECIPES

Santa's Favorite Cranberry Walnut Oatmeal Cookies

1¼ cups firmly packed light
   brown sugar
⅓ cup milk
1 teaspoon grated orange peel
1 cup all-purpose flour
½ teaspoon salt
1 cup dried cranberries

¾ cup shortening
1 egg
1½ teaspoons vanilla
3 cups quick oats, uncooked
½ teaspoon baking soda
¼ teaspoon cinnamon
1 cup coarsely chopped walnuts

Preheat oven to 375° F. Spray baking sheets with nonstick cooking spray. Place brown sugar, shortening, egg, milk, vanilla and orange peel in large bowl. Beat at medium speed until well blended. Combine oats, flour, baking soda, salt and cinnamon. Add to shortening mixture; beat at low just until blended. Stir in cranberries and walnuts. Drop rounded tablespoons of dough 2 inches apart onto prepared baking sheets. Bake 10–12 minutes or until cookies are lightly browned. Cool 2 minutes on baking sheet before removing to rack to finish cooling.

Yields: 2½ dozen cookies

Nutrition Facts

Serving Size 2 cookies (71g)

Amount Per Serving		
Calories 292	Calories from Fat: 150	
	% Daily Value*	Vitamin A 0%
Total Fat 16.7g	26%	Vitamin C 2%
Saturated Fat 3.8g	19%	Calcium 3%
Trans Fat 0.0g		Iron 8%
Cholesterol 11mg	4%	
Sodium 130mg	5%	
Total Carbohydrates 31.3g	10%	
Dietary Fiber 2.8g	11%	
Sugars 12.6g		
Protein 5.6g		
*Based on a 2,000-calorie diet		

Jody's Chewy Brownie Chocolate Chip Cookies

1½ cups firmly packed light brown sugar
⅔ cup butter
1 tablespoon water
1 teaspoon vanilla
2 eggs
1½ cups all-purpose flour
⅓ cup unsweetened cocoa powder
½ teaspoon salt
¼ teaspoon baking soda
2 cups (12 ounces) semisweet chocolate chips

Preheat oven to 375° F. In a large bowl, beat brown sugar, butter, water and vanilla at medium speed until well blended. Add eggs, beat well. In a separate bowl, combine flour, cocoa, salt, and baking soda. Add to shortening mixture, beat at low speed just until blended. Stir in chocolate chips. Drop rounded tablespoons of dough 2 inches apart onto ungreased baking sheet. Bake 7 to 9 minutes or until cookies are set. Cool 2 minutes on baking sheet before removing to rack to finish cooling.

Yield: 3 dozen cookies

Nutrition Facts		
Serving Size 2 cookies (64g)		
Amount Per Serving		
Calories 280	Calories from Fat: 133	
	% Daily Value*	Vitamin A 5%
Total Fat 14.8g	23%	Vitamin C 0%
Saturated Fat 9.1g	45%	Calcium 2%
Trans Fat 0.0g		Iron 5%
Cholesterol 36mg	12%	
Sodium 142mg	6%	
Total Carbohydrates 36.7g	12%	
Dietary Fiber 2.2g	9%	
Sugars 26.1g		
Protein 2.1g		
*Based on a 2,000-calorie diet		

MRS. ADELSTEIN'S GOOEY CINNAMON ROLLS WITH CREAM CHEESE FROSTING
(A BREAD MACHINE RECIPE)

DOUGH:

6–7 ounces milk	1¼ teaspoons salt
1 egg	3 tablespoons butter (softened)
3 cups bread flour	¼ cup plus 1 tablespoon sugar
2 teaspoons active dry yeast	2 teaspoons ground cinnamon

Place milk, salt, egg, 1 tablespoon butter, flour, 1 tablespoon sugar and yeast in the pan of a bread machine. Process according to manufacturer's instructions for a dough setting. When complete, remove dough to a lightly floured surface. Roll dough into a 15x9-inch rectangle, spread with 2 tablespoons butter. In a bowl, mix ¼ cup sugar and cinnamon; sprinkle over butter. Roll up tightly, beginning at 15-inch side. Pinch edges to seal. Stretch roll to make even. Cut nine 1½-inch slices. Arrange in a greased 9x9x12–inch square pan, spacing evenly. Cover; let rise until double in size, about 40 minutes. Preheat oven to 375°F. Bake 25–30 minutes, or until golden brown. Cool on wire rack for 10 minutes.

FROSTING:

1 (3 ounce) package cream cheese, softened	¼ cup butter
½ teaspoon vanilla	1½ cups powdered sugar
	⅛ teaspoon salt

While rolls are baking, beat together 1 (3 ounce) package cream cheese, ¼ cup butter, 1½ cup powdered sugar, ½ teaspoon vanilla, and ⅛ teaspoon salt. Spread on top of warm rolls before serving.

Yields 9 rolls. (*Nutrition facts include both rolls and frosting.*)

Nutrition Facts			
Serving Size 1 roll (116 g)			
Amount Per Serving			
Calories 384	Calories from Fat: 123		
	% Daily Value*		Vitamin A 9%
Total Fat 13.6g	21%		Vitamin C 0%
Saturated Fat 8.2g	41%		Calcium 5%
Trans Fat 0.0g			Iron 13%
Cholesterol 54mg	18%		
Sodium 462mg	19%		
Total Carbohydrates 59.4g	20%		
Dietary Fiber 1.6g	1.6%		
Sugars 26.3g			
Protein 6.7g			
*Based on a 2,000-calorie diet			

ACKNOWLEDGEMENTS

As I sit down to write this, I am overwhelmed to realize how many people have had a hand in helping me make this book a reality. It probably all started with my mom, who wrote fractured fairy tales for me in second grade and made me realize that writing could be fun. Thank you, Mom. Thanks to my dad for always believing in me and supporting me in whatever I set my hand to do. To my precious sister, Linnéa, who has always been there encouraging and cheering me on. One couldn't ask for a better sister.

I will be forever grateful to have my husband Steve by my side on this incredible rollercoaster of a writer's life. He has stuck with me, encouraged me, endured the angst and frustrations of living with a writer, then often picked up the loose ends around the house so I could write a few more paragraphs. I love you, Steve.

I also want to thank my Crit Sisters: Ashley Ludwig for her constant encouragement and cheerleading; Joanne Bischof, whose sweet spirit and incredible work ethic have spoken volumes into my life; Beverly Nault for telling me again and again, "You can do this!" and somehow getting my fingers back on that keyboard even when I thought I couldn't write another word. Bev's edits have made this book much better than it would have been otherwise. You are all three amazing authors and priceless friends.

Many thanks also go out to Rebecca Farnbach and the Temecula Christian Writer's Critique Group. Your encouragement has meant the world to me.

But most of all, I want to thank Jesus Christ, my Lord and Savior, without whom there would be no Christmas.

If I have forgotten any names, please forgive me and know that I am most grateful for all who have helped me on my journey.

www.ingramcontent.com/pod-product-compliance
Lightning Source LLC
Chambersburg PA
CBHW020634130626
46552CB00003B/1223